TULSA TIMES

Merrill J. Davies

Other Novels by Merrill J. Davies

The Best Version of Alice (2022)

Becoming Jestina (2018)

Our Pebble in the Pond (2016)

The Truth about Katie (2013)

The Welsh Harp (2012)

© 2023
Published in the United States by Nurturing Faith Inc., Macon GA,
www.nurturingfaith.net.
Library of Congress Cataloging-in-Publication Data is available.
ISBN: 978-1-63528-228-3

DEDICATION

This novel is dedicated to my father, John S. Johnson (1907–1994). By most standards, he would not have been considered a successful man, but to me he was a hero. With very little education, he managed to provide our family with a comfortable home. He was a hard worker and always told my sister and me that if we got a good education, we could do whatever we wanted to do. He was the most generous man I have ever known, and he loved children. Although this is a work of fiction, I think it stays true to my dad's character and personality.

Acknowledgments

There are so many people that I appreciate for helping me put this story together. I can't actually list them all, but I want to list a few. First of all, my husband Bill and my good friends Martha Heneisen and Sharon McBrayer have been faithful readers for all my novels, and I appreciate them more than they will ever know. For *Tulsa Times*, I really appreciate the help the Tulsa Historical Society gave me in my research before and during my visit to Tulsa. The Tulsa Research Library also went above and beyond my expectations when I spent the day doing research there. I also appreciate my friend Lawrence Baines, who took time to read the novel and write an endorsement.

CHAPTER 1

APRIL 1929—DEARBORN, MICHIGAN

Naomi's hands shook as she put the key in the lock on her brother Jonny's apartment door. She almost dropped the key, and her reddish-blonde hair fell down around her face. She half expected him to be in the apartment when she entered, but when she pushed the door open, all was quiet.

As Naomi went from one tiny room to the other, she found no sign of Jonny—or Marilyn, for that matter—in the kitchen or living room. The apartment was similar to the one where she and her husband Harris lived, except a little older. It was in the same area, but not owned by the same people, and it faced in the other direction from theirs. The white wooden buildings all looked alike. Most of the occupants were employees of Ford Motor Company. When she and Harris had moved there, Naomi was excited that their apartment was close to Jonny's.

She clinched an envelope with the landlady's name and "Apt. #110" printed on the front, and a note that read "Take this key and this money to the landlady." It did not look like Jonny's handwriting, but it was hard to tell. She wondered why her brother had not given the key to the landlady himself. Had he been kidnapped? Probably not. A kidnapper would not have left money for the next month's rent. Why had he and Marilyn left? Was Marilyn even gone? If so, where was her key? Naomi remembered what she'd observed the night Harris had been late coming home. Could Jonny's leaving have anything to do with that?

Although Naomi was only a year and a half younger than Jonny, he seemed much older. She would never have agreed to come to Michigan if her brother had not been working here.

As she walked hurriedly through the apartment, Naomi wondered why she'd even come in. She just had this desire to see inside the apartment, since she assumed her brother must have either left or been taken away. What if he'd been murdered? On the bed she found a blue dress shirt with a pack of Lucky Strike cigarettes in the pocket. A pair of men's black dress shoes sat on the floor beside the bed. Naomi picked up the shirt and shoes and looked over her shoulder, feeling like an intruder or a thief. She stood there a moment and then put the items back where she'd found them. She wouldn't take anything. She was probably over-reacting, she thought. Jonny would return in a few days and look for them.

When Naomi was about halfway down the narrow stairsteps to the first floor, she saw #110 on a door below. Approaching the door, she looked at the envelope, noting that it did not have Jonny's name on it anywhere. She quickly knocked on the door and after a few seconds, heard shuffling inside. A gray-haired lady cracked the door open just a bit and asked what she wanted.

"I have an envelope for you. It was left outside my door." Naomi held the envelope up so the landlady could see it.

The old lady opened the door a little wider and stared at her name on the envelope. "Well, who is it from?"

"I don't know," Naomi answered, handing the envelope to the lady. She hated to lie but could see no harm in not telling her. The envelope had not been sealed when she had found it outside her door, and Naomi had sealed it herself. The key had Jonny's apartment number clearly marked on it so she'd know he had sent it when she opened the envelope.

Saying goodbye as quickly as she could, Naomi hurried off, feeling like some sort of criminal because she had gone into Jonny's apartment instead of just taking the key and money to the landlady.

When she arrived back at her apartment, Naomi checked the time. It was still an hour before Harris would be home for lunch. She had made them peanut butter sandwiches before she had found the envelope and gone over to Jonny's apartment. She sat there thinking about what it all meant, wondering if she should have gone into the apartment. What if someone found out and blamed her for doing something more than just looking around? She hadn't even thought about that. She sat there for some time before she heard Harris turn the key in the lock.

When he entered, Naomi faked a smile and asked how his morning had been. Apparently, he noticed that she was not her usual self.

"What's wrong, Honey?" he asked.

"Nothing." She wasn't ready to discuss what had happened that morning, and if Harris wasn't aware that Jonny was gone, she wasn't going to tell him. He'd learn soon enough.

"Aw, come on, tell your sweetheart what's making you look so sad," he begged, encircling her in his arms. "All you need is just a little lovin'—isn't that right?"

No, no, no, she thought, pulling out of his grasp and going to the table to uncover the sandwiches she'd made. Finally, when lunch was over and Harris had returned to work, Naomi was able to relax and let the tears she'd held back spill over and flow down her cheeks. Although she knew no reason to blame her husband for Jonny's disappearance, somehow she did. Maybe the fact that Jonny had gone made her not trust men in general. What if Harris left too?

Naomi needed to get a plan for her life, just in case. She had always loved to sew, and her older sister had given her a sewing machine for a wedding present. It wasn't a new one, but it still worked well. Who knows? Someday she might be able to sew for other people. She went to the closet and brought out the machine. She found some blue and white fabric she'd bought just before they'd moved to Michigan, and she had thread of almost every color. What could she make out of the fabric? She began to look through some patterns she'd purchased, and before long she was feeling a little better, deciding to deal with her problems later.

Before Harris got home that evening, Naomi put away her machine and sewing materials and prepared dinner for the two of them.

While they were eating, Harris looked up at Naomi and asked, "Have you talked to Jonny today?"

"No… Why?"

"He wasn't at work. I was just wondering where he was."

Something about the way he looked at her made Naomi uneasy. She couldn't put her finger on it. "He might have been sick or something," she suggested. "I don't know."

"I'll check on him tomorrow," offered Harris.

In the coming days he made no mention of Jonny, which seemed odd to Naomi, but for some reason she did not want to talk to him about it.

In the next few days, she didn't see her sister-in-law Marilyn anywhere, so she had begun to think maybe she'd left with Jonny. Naomi's first thought had been that they'd had a fight and he'd left her. That would have been fine with Naomi; she'd never liked Marilyn anyway. But now that it had been several days and neither one had been seen, Naomi thought maybe they'd both left.

About a week and a half after Jonny left, there was a knock on Naomi's door. When she opened it, there stood Marilyn.

"Do you know where Jonny went?" she asked before Naomi said anything. It was more like a demand. Marilyn looked a little out of sorts and worried. She was wearing one of her usual prissy-looking, pastel-colored dresses.

"No, I don't," Naomi answered truthfully. She couldn't decide if Marilyn believed her or not, and it didn't really matter. She waited for a response. "Why?" she asked.

"Do you know when he left?"

Naomi hated to be questioned like this. She was surprised it had taken Marilyn so long to ask the question, though.

"I know nothing about it," Naomi replied, though this was not quite true. "You're the one who lives with him. You should know when he's home and when he's not. You tell me when he left."

To Naomi's surprise, Marilyn broke down and started crying. "I haven't seen him since last week. We had a big fight, and he left. At first I just thought he'd gone to stay with a friend for a night or so, and I didn't worry." Her sniffles continued, but she didn't say anything for a bit.

Naomi's first inclination was to ask what the fight was about, but she didn't want to hear the answer anyway, so she asked, "Have you contacted any of his friends?"

With this question, Marilyn's sobbing became worse. "Yes, but they haven't heard from him, and he hasn't been at work this week." Her blonde curls had fallen in her face, and as she sobbed, her hair became filled with tears and snot, but she didn't seem to care.

Naomi looked at her, remembering the first time she'd met Marilyn. Jonny brought her home with him one evening. Naomi was helping her younger brothers with their food at the table. As usual, they were rather messy. Marilyn never said a word to the little boys. She just looked at them with disgust, as if she were afraid she'd get dirty if she got too close to them.

"Do they make this big a mess at every meal?" she'd asked.

"Pretty much," Naomi answered.

"Somebody needs to teach them how to eat," Marilyn said in disgust.

Naomi had felt embarrassed for her little siblings—and for her mother, Julia—but she had also felt angry at Marilyn. As time went on, Marilyn had talked to the children a little, but she never really embraced them. Jonny would always kid around with them and make them laugh, but they'd never paid much attention to Marilyn, nor she to them.

It wasn't long after Jonny and Marilyn married that they moved to Michigan, where Jonny got a job in the Ford factory, so Naomi had little contact with Marilyn.

The next year Naomi and Harris had married. He was working at a store as a manager over the other employees. Naomi was proud of what he did and thought he would be a success. Not long after they married, however, the owner of the store had let Harris go, saying he didn't need him anymore.

"Did he tell you why he didn't need you?" Naomi had asked.

"He had his own ideas about what I should be doing, I guess. I was not going to wait on customers too. He was treating me like one of the other clerks."

Harris had been devastated, but there was nothing he could do. Naomi did not question him further, but it appeared he was fired because he refused to do what the owner asked him to do. He looked for other work for several weeks, but couldn't find anything. Harris always seemed to think he was just a little above most people, maybe because he had always had anything he wanted.

One week when Jonny was home for the weekend, he told Harris he would recommend him for a job with Ford in Michigan. Harris was excited, and even though Naomi did not want to move, she ended up agreeing to go because Jonny was there. Now Jonny was gone, and here was Marilyn, crying because he'd left her.

"Well, I'm sorry, but I really don't know where he is," said Naomi.

Heaving a big sigh, though not of relief, Marilyn continued: "The worst part is that today I saw my landlady, and she said she'd received an envelope from a stranger that had his key and our next month's rent in it. That means he's really gone." Marilyn continued to sob uncontrollably, occasionally looking up to see her listener's reaction.

If it had been any other person in the world, Naomi would have had the urge to put her arm around her and comfort her. In this case, however, she didn't feel much sympathy. She kept remembering the first time she had met Marilyn and the way she'd treated her little brothers. She blamed Marilyn for whatever had happened to her brother.

Three weeks later, Naomi had almost finished making a dress from the blue and white fabric she'd found. She had worked slowly and cautiously, one step at a time. She had decided to work at learning all the best ways to sew garments by reading different hints and explanations in the sewing book she'd brought from home. The book told her all about things like basting, hemming, lining, and sizing. It was an old book, and her mother had told Naomi she could have it in case she needed to look up something. And this week she had—almost every day.

The sewing made Naomi feel worth something, like she could do something good, maybe even make a living. She had not told Harris about her sewing. She wasn't sure why, but just hadn't. For some reason she thought he might not approve. She could be wrong, but this was something she didn't want to share with him.

Just as she had put everything away that day, Harris burst through the door as if he'd been shot out of a cannon. "Damn, damn …!" He was almost shouting.

"Wha…" Naomi started to speak, but he cut her off.

"The crazy guy fired me!" he said. "What am I supposed to do? I show up to work every day, don't I? I bet they can't find anyone any better!" He was pacing around the room like a caged lion. The little curl of black hair, which he normally kept carefully combed and neat, fell down over his forehead in a disheveled heap. Naomi was speechless and almost fearful. She had never seen him like this. She felt sick to her stomach.

Naomi believed they'd only hired Harris because he was Jonny's brother-in-law. He had lost jobs in the past because he didn't like to do as he was told. Jonny was a hard worker and had recommended him. Even though Harris was her husband, she knew he was not the kind of worker Jonny was. She kept quiet and listened to his ranting. Eventually he calmed down a little and said he'd look for another job the next day.

Without much conviction Naomi said, "You'll find something else—maybe even better than that job."

In the next few days Harris left each morning with a list of places where he planned to apply for work. Naomi was just glad when he was out of the house so she could get to her sewing project. After a week or so, however, he became frustrated and somewhat despondent.

About the time Harris had lost his job, Naomi had started feeling sick every morning. At first she thought it was because she was so worried about what they were going to do with Harris out of work. She was happy when, after several weeks with no luck finding a job, Harris announced that he'd decided to go back to Kentucky and try to find work there. She had begun to think she might be expecting a little one, and she wanted to be near her mother if she was indeed pregnant.

Chapter 2

Naomi's brief letter to her mother, saying that she and Harris were coming back home that weekend, had not mentioned Jonny. Nor had it mentioned the fact that Harris had lost his job and they were actually moving back to Kentucky.

She felt a little anxious about both Jonny's disappearance and Harris' job loss. She knew Jonny usually sent his mother a little money each week. Lord knows their mother needed it. Naomi and Harris never sent her any money. She had mentioned it once, but Harris said they didn't have any extra to send. He was a little like Naomi's dad, Hobert, who never had much luck in keeping a steady job. She wondered if Jonny had written to their mother. If he hadn't, she knew that would be the first thing her mother would ask about.

After sending the letter to her mother on Monday, Naomi and Harris had spent a few days getting ready to leave their apartment. They gave a few things away to their neighbors, trying to make their belongings fit into their car and a small trailer. Finally, it was Friday, and they were driving home. They had worked late the night before, packing as much of their stuff as they could get into the car and the trailer—and even tying a few items on top of the car. They only had a few things to do this morning, such as turning in their keys to the landlady. Naomi debated whether she should go over to the other building and tell Marilyn they were leaving; in the end, she just couldn't do it. Marilyn would have to figure things out on her own—unless Harris had seen her and told her his situation. In one sense Naomi was excited to be moving back home, but it also seemed like a failure.

The little road going out from London, Kentucky, was narrow, and traveling down it seemed to take longer than Naomi had remembered. The closer they got to home, the more anxious she became. Naomi knew her mother would know the story when she saw the car loaded down and pulling the small trailer. The little white house looked quiet, but before Naomi and Harris could get out of the car, Julia was out in the yard and talking to them.

"I have not heard from Jonny the last two weeks. Do you know why he hasn't written?"

In the short time between the question and her response, Naomi knew she probably betrayed something, but she wasn't sure what her mother thought. It was probably better to get it out in the open, though. What could she say?

"He hasn't written?" Naomi asked.

"No, I haven't heard a word," her mother replied. "Have you seen him recently?"

"Not this week," Naomi answered with certainty. She squirmed slightly, hoping not to look like she was lying. She walked on, with her face aimed toward the porch. She really wasn't lying: she had not seen Jonny this week. Her mother kept talking.

"You know he's been sending me a little money for the kids all along, ever since he started working up there." By the time they reached the porch, Julia was bearing down on Naomi, looking her straight in the eye. "It's been two weeks now since I've heard from him. Do you know if he's lost his job or anything?"

Julia was small, but she was a strong person, and Naomi knew she would not stop until she got some answers. So, she calculated what to say. Finally, she stammered, "Uh, I don't know. I haven't talked to him for about three weeks now. Harris lost his job. That's the reason we decided to move back here." That would get the conversation going in another direction, she hoped. Unfortunately, her mother wasn't so easily deterred.

They all sat down on the big porch. Naomi and her mother took the porch swing, and Julia continued her questioning. "So, you don't know about Jonny? Did you not tell him you were leaving?" Julia knew something was wrong. One didn't fool her easily. It was obvious that both she and Hobert, Naomi's dad, were concerned about their son.

Harris then spoke. "Ah, you know Jonny. He's always out partying, and we just got busy and didn't think of it before we left."

Naomi gave him a disgusted look. Harris would never be the man Jonny was. Jonny was hard-working and had always tried to help his mother as much as he could.

Julia stopped prying and went inside to prepare supper while Naomi and Harris unloaded the car. Where in the world would they put all that stuff? Naomi tried not to be angry, but she was very disappointed in her husband.

The next morning, while Harris and Hobert were outside doing some chores, Naomi came into the kitchen where Julia was making breakfast. She was stirring the eggs in one pan and frying bacon and sausage in the other. The smell of biscuits baking in the oven was evident.

"Mom, I don't know much, but Jonny has left Michigan, and I don't know where he went."

"What about Marilyn? Did she go with him?"

"No. He left her."

"What? What will she do?" asked Julia, with a concerned look on her face.

Naomi didn't know what to say, so she didn't answer for a few moments while she collected her thoughts. Finally, she sighed. "She did say he'd paid the rent for the next month, so that'll help. She'll probably have to get a job or come back home and stay with her parents."

"Did you tell her you were coming back?"

"No."

"And he just disappeared?" Julia seemed alarmed. "Jonny has always been so responsible. Are you sure he is okay? Could someone have killed him or taken him away? I can't imagine him leaving without telling anyone."

"I don't know for sure, but it seems to me if he paid Marilyn's rent for the next month, it means he went away of his own accord. And she did say they'd had a fight the day before he left," added Naomi. She hated for her mother to be thinking something bad might have happened to Jonny.

Julia did not push the subject of Jonny any further that day. Naomi expected that someday the truth would come out—but, then, maybe it wouldn't. A sadness pervaded the air as her mother started down the hall singing her favorite hymn:

> *I come to the garden alone,*
> *While the dew is still on the roses,*
> *And the voice I hear, falling on my ear,*
> *The Son of God discloses,*
> *And he walks with me, and he talks with me,*
> *And he tells me I am his own.*
> *And the joy we share as we tarry there,*
> *None other has ever known*

When Monday came, Harris set out to find a job. He had several leads but nothing definite. He spent all week looking, but by Friday he still had not found a job.

On Saturday morning Naomi suggested, "Well, there's always the coal mines. Have you thought about that?"

"You know I hate mining," he fired back.

"I know, but you've got to find work. Mama can't feed all these kids and us too." Sometimes she wished she could find the courage to leave him, but at least she could push him to get a job and support them.

"I know. I'll find something soon. I promise."

As she had the last few days, Naomi just didn't feel like saying more, so she walked back to their room. She sat on the edge of the bed until the sick feeling subsided, and then she started to unpack some of their belongings.

Over the weekend Julia sought her out early that morning and asked, "Naomi, are you not feeling well? Every morning this week you have acted like you couldn't eat a thing, and I thought I heard you heaving this morning before you came to the kitchen."

"Mama, I think I might be expecting a little one. I've felt sick every morning, and I did throw up this morning, but I feel better now."

"Oh, child, I know about that 'morning sickness,' as they call it. Yes, you may as well prepare for a little one to arrive in a few months. You will feel better after a couple months, though."

On Monday, Harris was back out job-hunting again. When they were alone, Naomi said to her mother, "Mama, I've been practicing my sewing on that sewing machine a lot lately, and I was wondering if I might be able to sew for other people around here. What do you think?"

"I think it would be great, Naomi!"

"What if I start by making one of the little ones something, and then we could show them off and offer my services to other families. Do you have any fabric?"

"Maybe. Let me look upstairs in that trunk."

In a few minutes her mother returned with two pieces of fabric that she thought might work.

"I think you could make Mark a shirt out of this," she said, holding up a piece of tan-colored fabric. "I even found a little pattern up there that might fit him."

"I think it would be perfect!" said Naomi.

The rest of the day Naomi and Julia plotted and planned about how they might make a little money to help feed the family by sewing for people. That night they told Hobert of their plans. He was all for it, but when Naomi mentioned it to Harris, he objected. He seemed offended that a woman might be able to make a contribution to the family income when he couldn't, but the two women shut him down quickly. The next morning he went off to work in the mines. As for the women, they were glad to get him out of the house.

Naomi spent the rest of the week making some display clothes for her little brothers, using the two pieces of fabric Julia had found, plus a few scraps from some of Naomi's old dresses.

"What do you think of this?" Naomi asked her mother one day. She held up a tiny dress she had made from the skirt of a pink and white dress she'd bought just before her wedding. She had spilled some tomato juice on the top of the dress about a year ago, and had been unable to get the stain out of it.

"Oh, Naomi, that's really cute. I remember that dress. Why did you cut it up, though?"

"Oh, I ruined the top because I spilled something on it, but there was plenty of fabric in the skirt."

"Maybe if the baby is a girl, you can let her wear it. But then, someone may want to buy it," Julia said.

Sewing every day made Naomi happy. By the end of the week, she had made two shirts, two pairs of shorts, and a little girl's dress.

Chapter 3

The trip had been exhausting. Jonny had no idea how far he'd driven. He had stopped several times in the evenings at dusk, pulled over on the side of the road, locked his car doors, and fallen dead asleep. Once he had seen a sign for a small motel in a little town and had slept there, but he didn't want to spend much money. Finally, he saw a sign for Tulsa, Oklahoma. He remembered something he'd heard about Tulsa being the "oil capital" of the world. Surely there was work there.

Late in the afternoon Jonny saw a sign that read, "Route 66 to Tulsa," and soon he was seeing signs that indicated he was close to Tulsa. When he entered the city limits, he knew he'd find some work. He just sensed that this was where he wanted to be.

When he stopped at a little store to get something to eat and drink, he approached the clerk. "Are there any rooms for rent or some place a fellow could at least sleep for a night or two around here?"

"Sure. You're in luck. There's a little motel just about a mile on that way." He pointed down the road. "See that blue sign? It will tell you the name of the motel. When you get there, tell them I sent you."

Jonny thanked the store clerk and headed that way. The lady in charge checked him in, and he unloaded the things he'd need for the night. He told her he'd be there a few days until he could find work.

As he settled in for the night, he felt good. For the first time since the "incident" with Marilyn, he felt like he was about to begin a new life. His whole life had been one calamity after another—or at least that's the way he saw it.

When Jonny was about nine years old and in the third grade, his dad lost his job. The next week he heard his mother crying in the middle of the night. He went into her room, but she wasn't there. He walked out to the porch and found her sitting on the swing and talking to someone. When he asked her who she was talking to, she responded, "I'm talking to the Lord, Son."

"Did he answer you?" he inquired.

"Well, not yet, but he will," she assured him.

"What are you talking about?"

"I'm just telling him that we're having a hard time, and I need some help feeding you kids."

"Maybe I can help," he offered. "What can I do?"

"I don't think there's anything you can do. Your dad needs to find work. I hope he will soon. That's what I'm talking to the Lord about."

The next day after school, Jonny heard his mother and father arguing. He heard his dad say, "Well, he could help with the hay and the vegetables and the other crops."

"But he's only nine years old. He needs to be in school," he heard his mother say.

"We've got to eat, though," his dad reminded her.

The next day when Jonny got home from school, he was told he would be working during the day instead of going to school.

"You mean I won't go to school at all?" he asked.

"No, Honey," his mom said, looking sadly at his dad. "Your dad needs you to help with the animals and planting corn and vegetables."

In a way, Jonny was glad. It made him proud to be of help to his parents and to be needed. His mother woke him up early the next morning, and as soon as he finished his breakfast, she sent him out to the barn where his dad was feeding the cows. His dad was a man of few words. He would just tell Jonny what to do and then walk on to do his own work.

Jonny soon learned the morning routine of feeding the animals and then going to the fields to plant, hoe, rake, plow, or whatever else his dad assigned to him. Some days, though, he would see his friends on their way to school, and he would miss being with them. One day they stopped when they saw him and asked, "When are you coming back to school?"

"I'm not sure," Jonny replied hesitantly.

He missed playing with the rest of the kids, but tried not to think about that. They were just kids, and he was an adult who helped his family. When school was out, he would often see kids out playing ball or going fishing, and he envied them for their freedom, especially as it got hotter in the summer months. Before long, his friends were back in school, and the work became a little different as Jonny helped with harvesting the hay and corn.

As time went on the next few years, he realized that the boys and girls who were in school looked down on kids like him who were not learning to read and write. He'd hear little comments at church or in town that made him feel like he was below the other kids.

"You're the boy who can't read, aren't you?" a boy said to Jonny when he was about 13 years old.

"I can read," Jonny said. "Maybe not as well as you can, but I can read."

One day he heard his mother tell his dad: "We may have to put Jonny back in school. Some people say children shouldn't be working until they get their education," she said.

"But Jonny's already 15. They're talking about those 12-year-olds who are working," said his dad.

"But he was working when he was nine," his mother said, "so he missed out on a lot of education."

And so it went, and Jonny was feeling worse about himself each year. When he was 16, his dad let him go to work in the mines in Harlan, Kentucky, a little farther east. It was common for kids to work in those days, although there was the beginning of a movement to restrict children from working.

Jonny was happy, working and making some good money, and he'd take his money home to his folks every week. His dad had a bad back, and he would get a job and then either quit or sometimes get fired because he worked too slowly. He even worked in the mines a little, but he didn't last long. Jonny would often be embarrassed at his dad's attempt to justify how slowly he worked or when his dad refused to do something because his back hurt.

Meanwhile, Jonny was building a reputation as a hard worker. "The best worker we have," his bosses would often say. Spending a lot of time lifting and hauling was building up his muscles, and that made him proud. He'd often be asked to demonstrate how to load the coal or lift a mine prop.

When he was 18, he heard that Ford Motor Company in Michigan was hiring workers. An older friend of his who worked there told Jonny he would help him find a job if he wanted to move there.

"That's a long way off," said his mother when Jonny told her about it.

"And you don't know anyone much or have any family up there," his dad added.

"But I could make more money," Jonny argued.

His parents were not happy about it, but when they saw that he really wanted to go and try it, they relented. His first year in Michigan was a year of fun for Jonny. He and his buddies went to bars every weekend that they didn't go home and sometimes in the evenings during the week. He loved the feeling of freedom. Most weekends they'd drive back home on Friday night and return on Sunday evening.

Jonny's parents had heard enough from his friend's parents to know that Jonny was imbibing too much alcohol and often getting into fights in bars. They were concerned. Their friends would say, "We need to find him a woman to marry, to settle him down a little."

One day Hobert was talking to his friend Tom Webb, a car dealer who had stopped by to visit. Jonny was home that weekend, and he heard Tom say to Hobert, "You know what Jonny needs? He needs a wife to settle him down."

"I don't know," said Hobert. "He's a good boy. He's just in with a rough crowd, I think."

"Of course," said Tom. "I know that. That's the reason I think he needs a wife. He'd settle down and behave if he had a wife."

By this time, Jonny was rolling his eyes. He couldn't believe they were talking about him this way. He'd find a girl one day, but he didn't want his dad to be talking to someone else about him.

"Maybe he would, but he isn't even courting anyone that I know of," he heard his dad say.

Tom thought for a moment. "You know, maybe we could get our kids together. My girl is just a year or so younger than Jonny, and she's been wanting to go out with the boys."

"Oh, I thought she was younger than that. Do you think she'd want to meet Jonny?"

"There's no doubt in my mind she would think he was something—just because he's a little older." That week Tom talked to his daughter and her mother, and it was arranged that Jonny and Marilyn should meet.

Jonny was not happy about the arrangement. "Dad, I can't believe you've put me in this position. And this girl… I don't know her, but I'm sure she feels the same way."

The day came, and they met. At first Jonny felt sorry for Marilyn, assuming she felt the same way he did, but when they talked a little, he realized she was not really against the idea of seeing him. He took her out to eat, and they had a good time.

So it was that when her parents said Marilyn was interested in Jonny, they all agreed it might be good if the two married. But none of the parents had considered what the young couple wanted. The two young people had merely done what they usually did: obeyed their parents and got married.

Jonny now accepted the fact that the whole fiasco may have been partially his own fault, but he could not go back. He was in Tulsa, Oklahoma, where he could start over and not make the same mistakes. He thought about Marilyn but did not let himself dwell on the past. He needed time alone to get ready for a brighter future. His eyelids were getting heavy. The first thing he needed was rest. Soon he turned off his light and gave in to his need for sleep. When he awoke, the sun was shining, and he felt ready to begin anew. He got up, bathed, shaved, and put on clean clothes for the first time in several days.

Jonny knew his first task was to get a job. He had never had a problem finding a job—or keeping one. Tulsa was a fairly big town and unfamiliar, of course. He began to ask anyone he met if they knew where he might find work. Most people said, "You might be able to work over there in the oil fields," or something like that. A few said, "Man, everyone's looking for work, but there's not much work to be found."

Tulsa was a bustling town in 1929, full of excitement. It really was the "Oil Capital of the World," according to the locals. When Jonny had left Michigan, he took only his clothes and a few other things, such as his radio (Marilyn had not wanted him to buy it anyway), with him. He had just bought a 1929 Model T Ford two months before he left. He had cashed his paycheck that Friday afternoon, so he had a little money with him but not enough to live on for long.

He decided that the oil companies were probably the best places to work, so a week after he arrived in Tulsa, he headed to Texas Oil to see what he could find. Even though the economic situation was bad all over the country, everyone kept telling him it would be easy to find a job just outside of town in the oil fields. After spending a few days looking, he found a job as a "roughneck" and a place to live, at least temporarily. He would be working 12 hours a day, six days a week.

The housing for oil workers was less than comfortable—more like tents in some cases—but he could live there for a while until he could save a little money. For the first several weeks he lived in those rather shabby conditions. He had three roommates, or bunkmates, and they too were hoping to get out of these temporary places as soon as possible. The work was hard, and the long hours made it seem even harder. After a few weeks, though, Jonny got a promotion of sorts, where his job was not quite as taxing. He continued to live in the cheap housing near the oil fields for a few months while saving enough money to rent an apartment.

One day a co-worker asked, "Jonny, didn't you say you wanted to get out of here and get an apartment soon?"

"Yes, I'd love to find something. This place is a dump."

"I know of an apartment house not too far from here. If you're interested, I'll take you over there one day and you can look at it."

"That'd be good," agreed Jonny.

"The only thing you might not like is that there's lots of kids over there. Some people have complained about that."

"Oh, I like kids, so that will not be a problem."

Jonny imagined that one day he might marry again and have his own children. Children fascinated him. It may have been because of his younger siblings, or it may have been his nature. In any case, he knew that having children around would not be a problem. As soon as he met the landlord and saw the apartment, he liked it. From then on, he continued to work hard and tried to make friends both at work and where he lived. Of course, some of the first friends he made at the apartment building were the children.

As soon as Jonny got off from work one day, he got in his car and drove to his little apartment to shower and change clothes. Walking by some kids playing in the street in front of the building, he swatted at one of them, danced around the group, and said, "You'd better watch out there, boys."

They laughed back at him and grabbed his arm as he swung one of them around and around. Jonny was not a big man, but his five-foot-eight frame made him seem big to the kids. He always played with them when he came back to the apartment building after work, and he'd often bring them a treat.

"Got any candy today?" one of them asked him.

Jonny loved it when they followed him around and talked to him. He felt in his pocket and pulled out a coin. "No, but here's a nickel. Go down there and get you some tonight when your dad gets home."

"Thanks, Jonny!" they shouted as he went inside.

Today he had plans to visit with Alex Smith. Jonny had met him at work soon after he had signed on at the oil field but did not know where he lived. Even though Alex was a good bit younger than Jonny, they seemed to think alike. Alex lived in town close to Cincinnati Avenue, one of the major streets that ran through Tulsa. His dad owned a grocery store in that area.

Jonny and Alex often went to one of the many bars or restaurants in Tulsa and mostly stayed out of trouble. Jonny thought Alex reminded him of himself a few years earlier, when he tended to be a little too hotheaded and drank a little too much. Alex's mother always said she wanted Jonny to "watch after Alex and make sure he doesn't get into trouble."

Jonny was glad she did not know his background, because if she did, she might not have entrusted her son into his care. Actually, it probably helped both of them, because Jonny could not imagine displeasing Alex's mother. She reminded him of his own mother. She was a short, pudgy woman, just like his mother, and her name was Julia too.

One day when Alex invited Jonny to come to his home after work, he said, "You can eat with us, and besides I want you to meet this guy that lives near my dad's grocery. He looks a lot like you."

"Really? You know someone who looks like me?"

"Well, I think he does. Anyway, he's married and has a little boy. He just moved in a few weeks ago, and I think he said he works at one of the oil rigs too, but I don't know where. Anyway, will you come? My mom says she'll feed us both."

"Well, I can't afford to pass it up then. You know how I like to eat. Will the guy be at your house too?"

"No, but he often comes by there on his way home from work, so you'll probably see him around the store."

That evening when he got off work, Jonny followed Alex up to the little grocery on East Young Street. He parked behind Alex, and they went into the store, where Alex talked to his parents and told them about his day. As they stood there talking, a young man walked in and asked for a couple items to take to "Ruby and the boy."

Mrs. Smith obliged. "Why sure, Mr. Hamilton. How is Ruby?"

While Mrs. Smith was getting the groceries, Alex said quietly, "Jonny, that's the guy I was telling you about—Jack Hamilton!"

Jonny looked at the man. He appeared to be a little older than Jonny, but he could see that there might be a slight resemblance between them. He walked over to the man and said, "Hey, this guy over here said you look like me! I hope you're not insulted by that."

"Well, no, I am not, but you may be," he said, laughing. "What's your name?"

"Jonny."

"Well, it's good to meet you, Jonny. I'm Jack. I've got to run on home. Ruby will be looking for me if I'm late. She can't finish making our supper until I get there."

When he left, Alex asked his mother, "Don't you think they look alike?"

"Yeah, I guess they do a little, although Jack seems a bit older. Maybe it's just because I know he's married and has a kid."

"How old is his little boy? Six?" asked Alex.

"Actually, Ruby said he is seven now. Cute little fellow," said his mother.

"They haven't lived around here long, but they seem like a nice family," said Alex.

Jonny always enjoyed spending time with Alex and his family. They were very different from his own family, though. Alex's mother and father had probably never been poor enough to worry about food, and now that they ran a grocery, they surely didn't. Alex had gone to high school and was considering going to college but just wasn't ready. He was working in the oil field until he could decide what he wanted to do. Jonny wished he'd had the opportunities Alex had as a child. He thought about the guy named Jack. He envied him. Jack looked like he had the perfect family. *Maybe one day I'll have a family, too,* Jonny thought to himself. Then he remembered what had happened with Marilyn. He didn't trust women much now. He'd imagined things would be great, but they weren't.

News on the radio in the coming weeks was filled with stories of a man named Charley Floyd, often referred to as "Pretty Boy" Floyd. He had robbed several banks, some of them in Oklahoma and some in other states. The last one had been in Ohio. He was on the "most wanted" list in several states.

It was about six months after his encounter with Jack Hamilton that Jonny thought about it again. One day after work Alex came up to Jonny and said, "Jonny, you're not going to believe this. You know that guy I introduced you to at my dad's grocery store? That was Charley Floyd. He's just living under the name Jack Hamilton."

"You're kidding me," laughed Jonny. "The one you thought looked like me? You think I look like a criminal?" *Well,* thought Jonny, *guess you can't trust men either.*

"Yeah, here it is all about him in this newspaper. My dad told me about it, and then a friend at work brought this paper to me this morning. Can you believe it? Look… It's definitely him."

"Yeah, it's him all right," Jonny said as he looked at the article. "Man, that's hard to believe. 'Pretty Boy Floyd'—I'd heard about him, but I never thought I'd meet him and not know who he was. They've been talking about him on the radio almost every day."

That evening Jonny walked into one of the bars, and a policeman was standing at the bar. Suddenly, the man turned and grabbed Jonny's arm. "What's your name, young man?"

"I'm Jonny… Why?"

"You look a lot like a criminal we've been chasing," the cop replied.

Jonny thought a minute. "You don't mean the Floyd guy, do you? They caught him already."

The guy behind the bar said, "He's right, Tim. It's here in the paper. You're right, though. He does look a lot like the guy."

Jonny couldn't wait to tell Alex about the incident. *Maybe Alex was right after all!* But he wasn't sure it was a good thing to be mistaken for a criminal.

The depression had not affected Tulsa as much as it had many other places. When Jonny had arrived in 1929, it was still booming with oil business. But by 1932, even Tulsa was feeling the effects of the joblessness around the nation, and jobs for people with little or no education were often cut out of work on a day's notice. Jonny had managed to hold on to his job, but several of his co-workers had been notified they were no longer needed.

Although Jonny had kept working, his daily hours had been cut back, and he no longer worked on Saturdays. He felt his days in the oil fields might be numbered. One Saturday he drove around Tulsa, trying to think of a job that might be more reliable.

Passing by a hospital, he thought about the fact that people got sick no matter what was happening. He decided to stop and ask about work there. When he went in and said he was looking for work, the first thing the man in charge asked Jonny was, "What can you do?"

"What do you need done?"

"Right now, we need someone to wash dishes."

"I can do that!"

"Could you help us out today?" the man asked in desperation.

"Sure."

After helping at the hospital on Saturday and Sunday, Jonny was able to begin the work full time on the following Wednesday after notifying the oil company he was leaving. The job was not easy, but it paid enough for his rent and food. He realized he was fortunate. Many people were out of work, hungry, and desperate. Also, the dust storms were awful. He had never seen anything like all that dust. You could see it coming from a long way off.

What bothered Jonny most were the long soup lines outside the hospital. He asked about them and learned that the hospital staff had been handing out small servings of soup and bread for several months. Some people thought they should stop, but the administration said they just couldn't do that.

Jonny started going out and talking to some of the people who were waiting in line. Many of them were women, mostly single mothers with small children. The children were usually dirty and hollow-eyed. They reminded him of his own mother and younger siblings, and it made him sad. He wondered what his own family was doing and how they were faring during this depression. But he couldn't do anything about that now. He vowed that if he ever married again, he would never leave his wife and children in the kind of poverty his own father had allowed his family to live in. Surely he could do better.

Each day when he took a lunch break, Jonny was drawn to those who were less fortunate. Maybe he could help these children in some way. In the fall, as the weather turned cooler, he expected the children would begin wearing shoes, but some of them didn't. When he asked one of the mothers where her children's shoes were, she hung her head and replied, "I just can't buy any this year."

"Maybe I can help you," he offered. "Will you be here tomorrow?"

"I try to bring the kids every day that I can, so yes, I'll probably be here most every day."

"I have a few dollars left over from my paycheck. I'll see if it's enough to buy them some shoes."

The pitiful woman seemed shocked. "Why are you doing that?" she asked.

"I'm not sure," he admitted. "It just seems like if I had kids that didn't have shoes, I'd want someone to help me."

He left the woman standing there in awe as he walked off. The next morning, as promised, he brought her two boys the shoes they so badly needed.

Chapter 4

Jonny had been in Tulsa long enough to feel at home. Michigan and Kentucky seemed far away to him, yet at times he felt a twinge of guilt. Every time he listened to the news on the radio or saw the newspaper headlines, the economic conditions of the country were the lead story.

Jonny was living quite well for an uneducated boy from Eastern Kentucky. In fact, now he had two jobs. After working at the hospital for a few months, he had gone back to working in the oil fields five days a week. He continued to work a part-time job at the hospital. Tulsa was a pretty good place to be as far as he was concerned. He was making enough money to live on and then some. The hospitals were overflowing with patients with lung problems because of the dust storms constantly blowing through, although it was not as bad in Tulsa as it was in the Panhandle area.

One Saturday morning as he was walking by the hospital, Jonny again noticed the soup lines with mostly women and children coming to get a little nourishment. It made him realize that if this had not been a booming oil town at the beginning of the depression, he might not have been able to find work as easily as he had. As he approached the line, he noticed the sad, dirty little faces of the children. He looked down at their feet. Just as he had seen earlier, most were still barefooted, although it was well past the time when they should have begun to wear shoes as the weather cooled off. He wondered what was happening to the little ones at home with his mother. With winter just around the corner, were they warm and safe?

He approached one of the mothers and asked, "Do they still do this every day?"

"Almost, yes. They give us a small serving of soup and bread. It gets us through the day. They've been doing it for several months now." She sighed, and she and her children moved up the line a little.

Jonny could see the faces of his little brothers as he looked at the children in front of him. It made him want to go back to Kentucky and check on his family. He couldn't forget the sad faces of one particular woman and her little boy and girl—twins, he thought. When he passed by a shoe store a few minutes later, he went in and bought two pairs of shoes that looked about their size. By the time he returned to the soup line, he had trouble finding the woman and her children, but eventually he saw them sitting on a curb eating their soup. He handed them the shoes. The children's eyes brightened, and they jumped up, almost spilling their soup. Amazingly, the shoes fit!

"Thank you! Thank you!" the woman and her children were all trying to say at once.

After that day, Jonny made many more trips to the soup lines on Saturdays, and he bought many more shoes that winter. Although it did not keep him from worrying about his own siblings, it did make him feel good to know he was helping someone.

On one of those Saturday excursions, as he was about to leave the area, Jonny saw a young lady who was talking to the parents also. She was bent down speaking with a little girl when he first saw her, and then she stood and spoke to the little girl's mother. He kept walking toward them. The young lady's hair was very dark, like many of the Sequoyah Indians he'd seen. By the time she finished talking to the woman, Jonny was close enough to talk to the young woman. She turned to look at him.

"What are you doing here?" the young woman asked, her eyes dark and fiery.

At first, Jonny was insulted by her question, even a little angry. His distrust of women led him to assume she didn't trust him either.

She seemed to sense his anger. "I just asked because I'm here with the Salvation Army trying to help children, and I thought you might be with them too," she explained.

He softened a little. "Oh, that's okay. No, I'm not with any agency. I just thought I might need to buy some of these kids some shoes. It's getting cold. I worked this week and made a little money."

"Do you know some of them?" she asked.

"No, not yet, but I feel for them. I grew up very poor, often needing things my brothers and I didn't have."

She seemed surprised at his words. "My name is Kitty," she stammered.

"I'm Jonny," he said. "Well, I've got to go now. I told three of the mothers I'd have shoes for their kids next Saturday."

As he left, he noticed one of the little boys looking at him. So, Jonny put his hand in his pocket and pulled out a piece of penny candy and slipped it into the child's hand. The little boy's eyes lit up, and he smiled. Jonny started walking off.

"Where are you getting the shoes?" Kitty asked as she turned toward him.

"I've bought several pairs down on Main Street. But this week I found some right down the street over there."

"I can't believe you're buying shoes for these kids. You must be a good person." Kitty looked astonished.

"Well, we can't let these kids go without shoes this winter," he said, as his little brothers' faces flashed before his eyes.

"I guess not, but I just don't know anyone else who seems to care so deeply," she said. "Do you live close by?" She seemed to be embarrassed to have asked him.

"No. I work here at the hospital part-time, though, so I often see them on the days I work."

"Well, I'll probably see you again because I'll be spending some time around the soup lines as part of my job. I don't know exactly what they want me to do, but I'm glad to have met you, and you have given me some ideas about what needs to be done."

As Kitty started walking toward the street, Jonny realized he'd missed the companionship of women. Kitty's words had broken through the barrier of his cynicism a little. Maybe all women were not like the woman who had betrayed him.

In the following weeks, he saw Kitty almost every week. Once he asked her if she wanted to come down to a little coffee shop with him. He had begun to think he liked her more than he should. The first time Jonny got a chance to talk to Kitty seriously, he felt it would be best to be honest with her and not give the impression that he was a single man.

"I'd best be honest with you: I'm a married man."

"Really? I've never seen you with anyone around here."

"That's because she's in Michigan—or maybe Kentucky—I don't know. Anyway, she doesn't live here."

"But you said you'd lived here for five or six years, so that doesn't make sense. When did she leave?"

"She didn't. I left her about five years ago."

Jonny began to tell her about how he was working late several nights a week and how she'd cheated on him. Once he got started, the words kept coming, and it seemed so natural. It wasn't hard to talk to Kitty. She sat quietly as he talked. When he finished, he looked at her with a questioning expression.

"Well, then, you've only got one more year. Then you can return to Michigan— or maybe Kentucky."

"What do you mean?"

"Well, aren't you just waiting your seven years so you can be legally free of her without a divorce?"

"I don't know anything about that. I just can't go back until…"

"The law says that after seven years they can declare you dead, and all legal obligations are over."

"But I don't know if they will do that or not."

A lot of questions had been left unanswered, and Jonny had not really told Kitty the whole story, but it felt good to talk about it a little anyway—especially with someone who seemed genuinely concerned and wasn't judging him or asking for a lot of information. He had not done that in a long time.

"You should get in touch with someone and find out—or ask them to get you declared dead."

Johnny knew he would not be accepted by family or friends as a divorced man. Would they accept him as a dead man?

Talking to Kitty had refreshed and renewed his faith in women. He had been badly hurt by what Marilyn had done, but he realized he needed to move on and find a way to deal with the old wounds, even if it meant taking some risks.

Sometime during 1934 or 1935, Jonny had started going to the dances at Cain's down on Main Street. The place was unlike anything he'd ever seen before. It had a spring-loaded maple dance floor designed in a log cabin pattern. Even if you weren't a great dancer already, it made you feel like you were. The first time Jonny went, he stood over to the side a while, but soon he just couldn't help getting out on the dance floor and giving it a try. Once he did, he was hooked.

Soon, he thought the best thing about Cain's was a man by the name of Bob Wills. He had a band called the Texas Playboys. Wow, could they put on a show!

The dance floor was crowded on a particular Friday night. Jonny had been there several times, and he was beginning to feel a little more comfortable trying to master his dance steps. Then a hush fell over the crowd, and the announcer said, "We'd like to present—the Texas Playboys!"

The crowd began to cheer, and five young men dressed in business suits, white shirts, and neckties appeared on the stage and began to play a familiar song. The dance floor became active again, and some young couples were singing along to the tune.

After the band played some songs, the announcer came back to the microphone and said, "And now, folks, our good friend Bob Wills."

Walking onto the stage was a young man in a tailored, double-breasted suit and polished, custom-made boots. The dance floor erupted again in wild applause as Bob Wills began to sing, "Take Me Back to Tulsa." Jonny had a perfect view of the performers. He was in awe of Bob Wills and his band.

Suddenly he saw Kitty just a few yards away dancing with someone. He had deliberately avoided getting to know the girls in Tulsa. Sure, sometimes he'd dance with the same girl twice, but once the dance was over, he'd scoot out quickly and not say much to anyone. As usual, he made sure Kitty didn't see him as the show wound down and he left the dance floor. He felt a little isolated. What does a guy do when he is married, but not to anyone near him?

Over the next weeks and months, Jonny saw Kitty a few times but never really talked to her. They just seemed to always show up at the same events. In some ways, she reminded him of his sister Naomi. He wasn't sure why. She didn't look like Naomi at all. Kitty had jet black hair and was considerably taller than Naomi. He thought it was because he felt so comfortable around her.

After Jonny left Michigan, he had not tried to contact anyone back home for the last few years. There was no way to get in touch with one person without risking everyone knowing where he was. He would have liked to have stayed in touch with Naomi, but he knew that if he contacted her, Harris would know too.

He would have liked to know what Marilyn had done. Had she stayed in Michigan or moved back to Kentucky? Also, he wasn't sure Naomi and Harris were still in Michigan either. He dared not write home.

He felt guilty about not sending his mother any money for the kids. In his mind, he could still see the little ones back home, and he could still hear his mother crying at night when everything was quiet. He could also hear her praying for his dad to find work and provide a way to buy groceries. But mostly he could hear her singing in the morning as she did her work. He could hear the words "I come to the garden alone, while the dew is still on the roses…"

Over the next few days, Jonny kept thinking about what Kitty had said, but he could not think of any way to get in touch with someone back home without letting them know where he was. One day as he was leaving after a shift at the hospital, he stopped to talk to one of the visitors.

"Do you have family here in the hospital?" Jonny asked.

"Yes. My father. He is very ill and has been for some time. I just came to visit a few days. I'll have to return to Georgia soon. By the way, my name is Donald."

"I'm Jonny."

Donald asked where he could find a decent place to eat. Jonny walked out with him and pointed down the street. "Just head down this street, go two blocks, and make a right. There's a little café about halfway down the block. The sign is in bright red letters. You can't miss it. They have good food."

As the man walked away, Jonny had an idea. "Hey, Donald," he said, "could I ask a favor of you?"

"Sure. What is it?"

"I need to mail a letter to Kentucky, but I don't want anyone to know where I am. Could I send it back to Georgia with you to mail?"

Donald paused for a moment, seeming surprised. "Tell you what, I'll do you that favor if you'll do one for me."

"That's fair," said Jonny. "What do you need?"

"I'd like you to visit my father on the days you work. I think he'd like you, and I'd also like you to write me a short letter each week while he's here and tell me how he's doing."

"I can do that," agreed Jonny.

"Okay. I'll be back around 10 in the morning, and we'll talk when you have time to come to my dad's room sometime during the day." He told Jonny his dad's name and room number, and a plan was made.

Jonny had to go home and decide who to send the letter to and what to say. He thought about all his choices. He was afraid if he wrote to his mother, the letter might be seen by someone else. Finally, he decided to send the letter to his sister Sue's husband, David. They lived across the county from his mother, and David had always been a good friend. Also, if someone in their family saw the letter, they wouldn't likely spread the news. Now, what to say in the letter? He needed to know if what Kitty had told him was true, but he couldn't learn that from here in Tulsa. He could not risk sending David his address yet. He began to write the letter.

Dear David,

I know you're surprised to hear from me, and I guess you're wondering where I am. I can't tell you yet. I am sorry for the trouble I've caused. I want to come home, but I can't yet. I want you to see if it is true that a fella can be declared dead after seven years and relieved of all his legal responsibilities. If it is true, I want you to encourage my family (or Marilyn) to declare me dead next year after August, but PLEASE DON'T TELL ANYONE ABOUT THIS LETTER! I'll write again in three months and tell you how you can let me know.

—Jonny

The next day, Jonny arrived in Donald's father's room just after lunch with the letter he wanted mailed. Donald gave Jonny the address he needed to send a report on his dad for the next three weeks. He promised to check in with Jonny when he returned to Tulsa.

For the next few weeks, Jonny visited Donald's dad every day he worked, when he had a break in the morning or at lunch time. Donald was right; his dad seemed to enjoy visiting with Jonny. They talked about all sorts of things, and Jonny even told him about leaving Michigan. He also told him about his work at the hospital and how he'd hoped to get a job with East Texas Oil Company in Tulsa. The old man said he had a friend that was "somebody" with East Texas Oil, and as soon as he could, he'd contact him to see if any jobs were available.

CHAPTER 5

When Donald returned to visit his father, Jonny learned he'd mailed the letter the same day he'd left Tulsa three weeks ago. He wondered what David had thought when he heard from him, and if he would try to find out whether seven years would be long enough to stay gone.

"Jonny, I want to thank you for keeping in touch about my dad," Donald said.

"How's he doing today?" asked Jonny,

"He's doing great, and I've got good news. He gets to go home Friday."

"Did he say anything to you about our conversation about looking for a job with East Texas Oil?"

"No. Do you mean you want to work for them?"

"Yeah. I was telling him that I work out in the fields, and he said he knew someone who might be able to help me get a better job with East Texas Oil." Jonny paused. "I hope I'm not out of line by asking about that."

"No, no. Actually, my uncle—my mother's brother—works for East Texas Oil. I think he has an important job with them, so he might be the one who could help you."

"Well, I'll do anything, and I'm okay working here at the hospital, but I like working outside, and working in the oil fields pays better."

"I'll probably see you before I leave, but thanks again for keeping me updated on Dad. He has really enjoyed talking to you."

"He's a good man, Donald. I'm glad he gets to go home."

"He has always been a good father to me and my brother. From what Dad says, you seem to have come from a good family too."

"Yeah, my parents are good people, although I wish my dad had been able to provide better for my little brothers and sisters. I used to send Mom some money along, but I haven't been able to do it these last few years."

"I don't want to be too nosy, but why did you leave Kentucky? I assume that's where you lived," Donald said. "You don't have to answer that, you know."

"Well, I guess I may as well tell you. I left from where I was working in Michigan, but all my folks are in Kentucky. The man I sent the letter to is my brother-in-law." Jonny had to stop and collect his thoughts before he went on. "I married a young girl, mainly because both my parents and her parents thought we should get married. They probably thought it would settle me down and be good for us both. Turns out she was cheating on me. I just kind of panicked. I knew all hell would break loose if I tried to divorce her. I also knew that if I told who she was seeing (another one of my brothers-in-law), it would devastate the whole family. So I just left without much of a plan."

"Wow! That's quite a story, Jonny. I admire you for the courage it must have taken to do that. Will you ever go back?"

"I don't know. I heard from someone that there is some kind of law that after seven years you can be declared legally dead if no one has heard from you. Next year will be seven years. I sent that letter to another brother-in law that I trust and asked him to check it out. They can't find me because it was mailed from Georgia, but I'll need to know if they declare me dead. Know what I mean?"

"Well, you're a bright young man. You'll figure it out, I'm sure. Keep in touch with me, and I'll put you in touch with my uncle. On second thought, I'll just give you his name, and I'll send him your name. Then you can just go out there and talk to him."

Jonny had become a little skeptical about people since his failed marriage, and he didn't know whether to expect anything from Donald's uncle or not, but he finally got in touch with him. After asking Jonny a few questions, he said they needed more roughnecks out at Glenn Pool. Jonny agreed to come the following Monday.

Jonny didn't know what to expect. He knew it would be hard work, but he could make a good impression there if he worked hard. He really wanted people to know that whatever he was assigned to do, he would do it better than anyone else. For the most part he always did. He liked being the best. He never wanted to be the supervisor on the job. He just didn't have the skills to read instructions and write up the reports.

When Jonny arrived at the refinery on Monday, he was taken to the tool pusher, who was responsible for all the crews. The guy looked stressed.

"Man, I need you in so many different places, I don't know where to start. I think I'll start with letting you help the motorman over here. Just do whatever he tells you."

It went like that all day. About the time Jonny got comfortable doing one thing, the tool pusher would come around and take him to another job. By the end of the day, the tool pusher told him he thought the motorman needed the most help and that he should report to him the next morning.

Jonny liked the job because every day was different. One day he was helping maintain a waterline, and the next day he might spend time assisting with maintenance on something else. What he liked best, though, was when he assisted in moving equipment on the site. The motorman had high expectations, but if you worked hard, he left you alone.

A few weeks after he started work there, Jonny saw one of the young men approach him from another crew.

"Don't I know you?" the young man said.

"I don't think so," responded Jonny.

"You look familiar. Have you ever lived in Michigan?"

Jonny's heart skipped a beat. "No, you must be thinking of someone else."

The man walked away, but Jonny couldn't stop thinking about it. What if the guy had seen him in Michigan? Was the young man communicating with someone back there, and would he get word to someone who knew Jonny?

In the next few days, every time the man saw him, Jonny thought he stopped and stared a moment. He tried to discount it, but he was bothered by the fact that the man seemed to be sure they'd met. One night as they left work, the man lingered along with Jonny and began asking him questions again. Jonny assured him that he was mistaken, but he wouldn't hush. The longer he talked, the angrier Jonny became.

Before he knew it, Jonny turned around and threw a punch at him—hit him right in the nose. Blood oozed out, and the man turned and punched him back. After a few punches, one of the other workers pulled them apart and told them to stop. The worker, who was a friend of Jonny's, told the man to go on and urged Jonny to wait until the man left the grounds.

After that, Jonny never saw the guy again, but he was bothered for several weeks by what the guy might know and whether he might be reporting something to someone. Finally, he got back into his work routine and forgot about the incident.

As usual, Jonny had worked a hard shift, but he felt good. He'd noticed that one of the supervisors was watching him as he completed his tasks, and when he finished, the fellow had asked him to come over to the side.

"Jonny, I see you working like a pro. How about coming in a little early in the morning. I'd like to talk to you about a job that you might like better, because you could help some of these fellows learn how to get the job done."

"All right. I'll be here early in the morning," Jonny answered.

The next morning, sure enough, the man was there. He told Jonny that he'd like for him to supervise the other five men on the crew. Jonny felt good about the new job as he completed the tasks.

It was late in the day when another one of the supervisors handed him a few papers and said, "Now each day you'll need to fill out a form on each of these men so we'll know how much work they get done."

As the man walked away, Jonny started sifting through the papers. He realized he might be in over his head. First of all, he wasn't sure he could spell the names of the five men. Also, he was unfamiliar with some of the words used in the instructions for filling out the forms. He was reluctant to ask the man to read the instructions for him, fearing the man might think he was stupid and not want him to continue in the job. He immediately had a bright idea for a solution to the problem with the names.

He walked over to one of the men and asked, "Do you know the names of all the men on the crew?"

"Yes," replied the man.

Jonny said, "Tell you what… if you'll write their names on these forms, I'll finish what you're doing. I hate to say it, but I don't know everyone's names yet."

"It's a deal," said the man, looking relieved to stop what he was doing.

Knowing that his problem was more than just not knowing all the men's names, Jonny struggled through the forms for a few days, finding ways to ask about what the instructions meant without openly revealing that his main problem was his limited reading ability. After about two weeks, the person who had hired him called him in.

"Jonny," he said, "you have been doing a good job with getting the work done on your shift. I appreciate that very much. However, I'm getting some complaints from those who are processing your reports. Do you know what the problem might be?"

"What's wrong with the reports?" Jonny asked, pushing the man to explain.

"I'm not sure I understand either," he said. "They say that sometimes your answers don't exactly match the questions."

"Well, I do the best I can. Sometimes I just don't understand what they want."

Jonny was such a hard worker that his supervisor apparently did not want to give up on him. For Jonny, though, it was embarrassing to struggle through every weekly report. Finally, after about six weeks of supervising the men, Jonny asked his supervisor if he could talk to him at the end of the shift.

"Sure. I'll see you just after you finish," the man said.

As Jonny entered the office at the end of the day, his supervisor looked up from his desk. "Thank you for talking to me," Jonny began.

"Of course, man. Anything for my best employee."

"I appreciate the vote of confidence, but I have a request to make. Could I just go back to being one of the workers? I don't want to be the lead worker. I just can't handle it."

"Why not?" asked his supervisor and friend.

"I just can't do it," said Jonny. "The actual work is okay, but filling out all these papers—I just can't do it."

"What is so hard about it?"

Jonny looked down and then back up at the man. "I'm sorry, but I only went to school for three years when I was a kid, and I just can't read very well. Does that make sense?"

"I understand. It does make sense. I thought something was wrong, but I just didn't understand what the problem was. Well, I really like the way you handle the job, but I have had a few complaints about the forms. I just thought it was their own fault, but if you really think you'd rather not continue as the leader, then I respect that decision. I certainly don't want to lose you as an employee."

"It's just too much for an old boy like me. I just want to do the work."

"Okay. I understand. Can you stay on in the position until Monday? I think I can find a replacement by then."

Jonny agreed and left with a mixture of relief and embarrassment.

Chapter 6

In the spring of 1935, Jonny was spending a lot of his money on attending events at Cain's Dance Academy. It was the place to be in Tulsa, especially in the evenings. He especially liked the nights when Bob Wills and the Texas Playboys were there. The place was rowdy, and there was a good bit of drinking.

Jonny learned that Bob Wills was from the small town of Turkey, Texas. He and his Texas Playboys first played in Fort Worth, but in January 1935 they played for the first time at Cain's in Tulsa, and Wills quickly became a favorite there.

Jonny had not seen Kitty for several weeks. Then one Saturday night she showed up at Cain's. She was laughing and seemed to be having a great time, just as he was.

"Do you like Bob Wills?" he asked her.

"Yes! I've mostly just heard him on the radio, though. This is only my second or third time to see him in person. My brother gave me tickets, and one of my friends had tickets too, so we came together."

As Kitty walked off toward her friend who was waiting for her, Jonny thought she seemed a little embarrassed. He thought Kitty probably did not want to get involved with the likes of him, and he couldn't really blame her.

Just as the crowd was getting tired of waiting for the show to start, a hush fell over the audience, a curtain was pulled back, and the announcer began to talk. A moment later the man said, "And now…I give you Bob Wills and the Texas Playboys!" Immediately, the group appeared, ready to entertain. The audience was obviously impressed. They clapped wildly and stomped and yelled as Bob Wills began to sing "Living on Tulsa Time."

By intermission, several people–including Jonny–were dancing along with the music. He looked around for Kitty but did not see her.

At the end of the show, the announcer came back to the stage, where he reminded the audience of coming events at the venue. "If you've enjoyed tonight, remember that Bob Wills and the Texas Playboys will be right back on this stage next Friday night! I hope to see many of you back here with us."

As he was leaving the show, Jonny saw Kitty up ahead of him. He hastened his steps a bit. "Hey, Kitty, how'd you like the show?"

She stopped and turned around. "I loved it!"

"Are you coming back next Friday night?" he asked when he caught up with her.

Kitty turned to him quickly. "I'm not sure. My brother gave me tickets for tonight, but I may come back on my own next week. I really liked the show." She went on to mention that she had saved a little money from her job.

Wow, a woman who can pay her own way, he thought. *That's impressive!*

"Would you consider letting me come by to pick you up?" The words were out of his mouth before he could stop them. Now, as he waited for her to answer, he thought he'd made a mistake. She walked a few more steps and then stopped and turned around.

To his surprise she said, "Sure, if you'd like. I just live about two blocks from here."

"Can I give you a ride home, then, so I'll know where you live?"

"Sure."

Jonny was relieved. As they walked to his car, they naturally started a conversation about the Bob Wills show they had just seen. She pointed the way toward her house as he started the car.

"Did you say you are working for the Salvation Army or volunteering?" he asked.

"I'm working for the Salvation Army now. I began by volunteering three days a week at a settlement house provided for the homeless. The work was so demanding, and I would be exhausted by the end of each day, but the stories I heard each day just made my heart hurt. Many of the people I met were heading out to California to find work. They came in droves, mostly driving trucks loaded with all their belongings. The adults looked hollow-eyed and hopeless; the children, with protruding stomachs, looked gaunt, often crying or just staring into space. It was pitiful."

"Yeah, that's what I see at those soup lines at the hospital. It's terrible."

"Anyway, one of the leaders asked me if I would consider working for them downtown here in Tulsa. At that time I was volunteering out at the settlement, working with people who were looking for jobs and did not plan to move on to California."

Kitty stopped for a moment. "Oops! I got so involved in telling you about my work that I've let you pass by our house. You'll have to turn around now and go back down to the end of the block. I'm so sorry!"

"It's no problem," he said. "I wanted to hear about it. It sounds like you're doing good work."

"Well, I'm just glad to have a job, even if it doesn't pay a lot. I really like the work too. I've had other jobs, like clerking at the grocery or the five-and-dime store, but I never enjoyed those like I do working for the Salvation Army. I feel like I'm in the right place. I want to learn more, maybe go to college and learn more about social work."

"I'm glad you'll let me pick you up next Friday night," Jonny said.

"Me too," she said. "I promise not to talk so much then and let you do the talking."

"That's all right," he said. "I've enjoyed it. I wanted to get to know you better. I'll see you next Friday."

The next week Jonny found himself counting down the days until he could take Kitty to Cain's to see the show on Friday. Each evening he stopped by the little store down the street and bought a few sticks of candy to give the kids in his apartment building. When he arrived home, they'd be standing around looking for him. The moment he opened his car door, three or four of the little munchkins would be looking up at him and pleading, "Jonny, what did you bring today?" And, of course, he'd always have something.

Jonny rushed home from work on Friday to get ready to go to Cain's, and he forgot to stop by the store. As soon as he pulled into his parking place at home, he realized he was in trouble. Three little faces were peering up at him as he stepped out of his car. Never one to make excuses, he decided to tell them the truth.

"Hey, Pie Faces," he said. "You know what? I forgot to stop by the store!" Their faces fell. Quickly he said, "I guess I'll just have to pay for it. I've got some money that you can use the next time you go to the store, and you can buy whatever kind of candy you want." Their faces lit up, and they began to smile. He put his hand in his pocket and pulled out three bright coins. "Look here," he said, "one for each one of you!" They grabbed the coins, and off they went.

As the children ran off, Jonny hurriedly went up the stairs to his apartment. It was the first time he'd taken a girl to a show or dance in a long time. He took a little extra time to get ready, and he actually stood in front of the mirror and debated over which shirt made him look better. Why? He wasn't sure. He was still a married man. He was still a man with no education and no prospects of getting one. All he knew was that it was important to him to look his best when he picked up Kitty this evening.

When he got to her house, he sat in the car for a few seconds and then went to the door and knocked. They stared at one another briefly, and then she said, "Oh, come on in. I want you to meet my mom and dad." As she turned around, both her parents entered the living room and spoke.

Jonny extended his hand and smiled. "It's great to meet both of you. I've enjoyed getting to know your daughter." They seemed welcoming enough, and thankfully they didn't mention anything Kitty had told them about him. He hoped she had not told them anything.

"How are you?" her mother asked.

"Dad," Kitty said, "Jonny works for East Texas Oil during the week and at the hospital on weekends."

"Oh," said her dad. "That's hard work in the oil fields."

"Yeah, it is," answered Jonny. "*Roughneck* is a good term for that kind of work. I had a lot of scrubbing up to do before I came tonight to look presentable."

"It's hard for anyone to look presentable lately," said her dad. "Have you noticed that there is a lot more dust here in the last few months?"

"I thought all those dust storms were only out in the Panhandle," said Kitty's mother. "The last few storms, though, have blown in so much dust that it's everywhere—on the porch, in the house, just anywhere you look."

"Yeah," laughed Jonny. "I picked up my plate to eat the other night, and it actually had dust on it before I got to the table." They laughed.

"I can believe that," said Kitty's dad.

On their trip to the show, which only took a few minutes, including parking, Kitty asked Jonny, "What's your favorite Bob Wills song?" She looked at him across the 1929 Model T Ford.

"'Take Me Back to Tulsa,'" he answered without hesitation. "Yours?"

"Not sure," she said. "I'll tell you when the show is over, but I do like 'Living on Tulsa Time.'"

That night the show seemed like the best Jonny had heard. The band sang all the favorites, including "Living on Tulsa Time," "Take Me Back to Tulsa," "San Antonio Rose," "Ida Red," "Faded Love," "Stay All Night," and "Corrina, Corrina."

A little before the show ended, Jonny asked Kitty if he could take her to get something to eat afterwards, and she agreed.

"Where do you want to go?" he asked.

"We could go over to Weber's," she said. He gave her a blank look. "You know, Weber's Superior Root Beer."

"Oh, yeah. That sounds good. I love root beer, and I've heard they have the best in town."

"And they have good hamburgers too," added Kitty.

"Then Weber's it is."

At Weber's they sat and talked for an hour. She learned about his family in Kentucky and what he'd done in Michigan. He also told her a little about his sister Naomi.

"Why are you working two jobs?" she asked.

"Well, just because I can, I guess."

"But aren't you exhausted by the weekend? Exactly what do you do at the hospital?"

"I do whatever they tell me to," he said with a grin. "Wash dishes. Mop floors. Clean out drains. I'll do anything."

"But why do you want two jobs? Isn't one enough?"

"Well, think about all those children who are hungry and don't have enough clothes for winter. If I work two jobs, I can help them more. That's the reason I like working at the hospital. I can make a little extra money and maybe buy a few more shoes."

"I am amazed at you, how you think. I've never met anyone like you before." She paused. "I guess I need to get home now."

When they approached her house, she told him that her folks might be asleep so she couldn't invite him in. To her surprise, though, she saw that her brother still had friends there, and all the lights were on. "It looks like I was wrong," she said. Come on in and meet my brother if you have time."

"I'd like to if you don't mind," he said quickly. "I miss my folks back in Kentucky."

When they went into her house, Jonny just fell right in with the others, talking and laughing and telling them about the Bob Wills show. They reminded him a lot of his own family. Soon he said he'd better get back to his place because he had to be back at the hospital early the next morning.

"Oh, that's right. You're not off on Saturdays," Kitty said.

"No, I'm afraid not. Hospital patients don't go home over the weekend," he said with a grin.

"Oh, I guess not. I'll see you around."

"Will you be at the soup line any next week?" he asked.

"Maybe," she said. "I just do what they tell me. They've been sending me over there on Tuesdays and Thursdays, but who knows?"

"Maybe I'll see you there then—that is, if you get to come on Saturday," he said before he left.

Jonny looked for her at the soup line the next week, but she didn't show up, or at least she was not there on Saturday. Maybe she was trying to avoid him. The next week it was the same thing—no sign of Kitty.

Chapter 7

Jonny was looking forward to the weekend when he got off work one Friday. Alex's mother had invited him to dinner. The Smith family had become his "family" in Tulsa. As he drove up Cincinnati Avenue, he was whistling a Bob Wills song. When he turned onto the street where the Smiths lived, he was surprised to see Alex and a young black man walking along the street near Alex's home.

"Hey, guys," he said.

Alex looked back and raised his hand. "Hey yourself," he said. "Pull on down to the house. I want to introduce you to my friend here."

Jonny did as Alex said, wondering who the young man was. It was unusual to see a black person in a white neighborhood in Tulsa. He remembered often seeing black people back in Kentucky, and even in Dearborn, Michigan, but here they seemed to keep to themselves much more. He remembered hearing something about a law that forbade black people from working for white-owned businesses, and he'd heard something about a neighborhood called Greenwood that had been torn down a few years back. It seemed like most people just didn't ever say anything about it, though. He'd asked someone one time, and they'd just said, "I don't know anything about what happened in Greenwood. My parents always told me not to talk about it."

When Jonny got out of his car and looked back down the street, he saw that Alex and his friend were almost to the house too.

"Jonny, this is my friend Berko. He and I have been friends ever since we were kids." He looked at his friend. "Jonny and I work together at East Texas Oil."

"Did you say your name is 'Berko'?" The young man nodded. "My name is Jonny. Jonathon actually, but everybody calls me Jonny."

"Yeah, Berko means 'first son'; I'm the oldest of three sons."

"Well, then my name should have been Berko too," laughed Jonny, "because I'm also the oldest son. Anyway, it's good to meet you."

They were interrupted soon by Alex's mother calling them in to eat a delicious meal. As they were finishing, Jonny looked at Berko and inquired: "So how did you and Alex get to be friends as children?"

Berko looked at Alex as if he wasn't sure how to answer. Alex said, "Go ahead and tell him our story, Berko."

Berko hesitated a moment. "Have you heard the story of Greenwood?" he began.

"Not really. No one seems to want to talk about it. I've asked, but people seem reluctant to discuss it."

Alex sighed. "Well, most white people are, because it was such a horrible thing they did to our community. They ought to be ashamed to talk about it, that's for sure."

"So, what happened?" asked Jonny.

They all looked at each other for a few moments. Then Alex's mother spoke. "Basically, we had a black neighborhood here in Tulsa that was very successful, with lots of businesses and services, and a bunch of white people tore it down, burned homes and businesses to the ground, and never were held responsible for it. Even the police—they did nothing. Well, I'd better hush because the more I say, the madder I get."

"When was that?" asked Jonny.

"It was in 1921," said Alex's dad. "Probably the only good thing that came of that incident was that we got to know Berko."

"So, my mom had to find work somewhere after my dad and little brothers were burned to death in the massacre," explained Berko.

"His mom asked my mom if she could bring Berko with her when she came to work in the store, and of course Mom said yes," said Alex. "Dad had gone over with a group to help in the days after it happened, and when they met Berko and his mom is when his mom asked if she could work in the store."

"At the time most of the white people in the surrounding communities wanted to pretend it was somehow Greenwood's fault, that someone had done something to cause all that destruction. But we always knew one person breaking the law, even if they did, would not be a reason to burn down a whole neighborhood. Anyway, Berko and Alex became fast friends during that time and always will be, I hope," said Alex's mom.

"That's terrible," exclaimed Jonny. "What did your family do before that, Berko?"

"My dad worked in a grocery store in Greenwood. At the time my mom was staying home with us kids, but after Dad died, she knew she had to find work, and there was just nothing there to do after so much was destroyed. Eventually, of course, some of the businesses built back, but that took a long time," he said.

Johnny could see the sadness in Berko's eyes when he spoke of his parents and siblings, so he didn't ask any more questions.

Chapter 8

One Saturday morning when Jonny was delivering shoes to two little kids in the soup line, he turned around, and there was Kitty, talking to some parents in the other line.

Kitty spoke to him, and they talked a little, but Jonny suspected she was a little afraid to get involved with him, and he could understand that. After that, he just focused on his work and tried to make some friends there. He was hoping he might be able to go back east eventually.

He continued to enjoy going to Cain's, especially on weekends, and one week said to Pete, one of his friends at work: "Let's go to Cain's Friday night. Bob Wills will be there."

"What's it like down there now?" Pete asked.

"Oh, it's the place to go in Tulsa. I go there a lot, on weekends especially."

"I've heard it's a very popular place now. I grew up in Tulsa and used to take ballroom dancing at Cain's when I was in high school, but I've never been to a show there," said Pete. "The dance floor is impressive. I remember that about the place. It feels like it springs up under your feet when you dance."

"Yeah, I love that dance floor."

"It's been there about five years and is very well known in Tulsa," said Pete. "Initially Tate Brady had the place built for a garage, but I don't think it was ever used for that."

"Who was, or is, Tate Brady?" asked Jonny.

"He was a big businessman and a politician. I think he was the founder of Tulsa, but he committed suicide sometime in the '20s. Anyway, a man named Madison Cain finally bought the building and made it into a place to teach ballroom dancing."

"So that's why it's called Cain's," said Jonny.

"Yes, it had been a club called the Louvre during the prohibition era, but it was never very popular until Mr. Cain bought it and called it Cain's Dance Academy. That's when it began to gain some popularity."

"It's definitely the most popular place in town now. I think Bob Wills is making it even more famous," said Jonny. "So, do you want to go hear Bob Wills and the Texas Playboys?"

"Sure," said Pete. "What time does it start?"

"I think it's seven, but I'm not sure. Why don't I meet you there a little before seven so we can find a good place to watch the show. I'll meet you at the entrance of the building."

There was a line of people waiting to get in when Jonny arrived on Friday evening, but it seemed to be moving fast. Pete had arrived at the same time he had, and they had their tickets ready to present when they reached the door. The band was playing, and people were already out on the dance floor. Suddenly Jonny saw a familiar face—Kitty!

"Hey there, girl! Where've you been?" he said.

Kitty turned and smiled. "I was at the soup line last Saturday. Where have you been?"

Jonny laughed. "I was there, too, but apparently not when you were. Wanna dance?"

"Of course," she answered.

Jonny was a smooth dancer, and Kitty was too. Both of them had come with a friend, but soon they had forgotten all about their friends, the crowd, and everything else. They were lost in the joy of the moment. They danced several numbers, and finally it was time for the official show to begin. "And now, Bob Wills and the Texas Playboys" the announcer said.

"I think this is my favorite song," Kitty said, as the band began playing "Living on Tulsa Time."

Just before the show ended, Jonny looked over and saw his friend Pete dancing with a girl he had not seen before. He nudged Kitty, "Oh, there's Pete. He's a friend from work. We met here tonight, but it looks like he's found a friend too—just like I did! I don't know her, though."

Kitty looked in the same direction as Jonny and started laughing. "Oh, that's my friend Maggie. We came together!"

They both laughed and walked toward the couple when the show was finished. "Let's go to Weber's and get a root beer," said Jonny when they met Pete and Maggie.

Chapter 9

As much as Jonny loved going to Cain's to hear Bob Wills on the weekends, he was also fascinated by the theaters. He loved the organ music at the Ritz–and one time even met the famous organist/pianist Milton Slosser while there. He liked the atmosphere there, too. He had never seen such a beautiful place, and he could just sit there and forget all about his work and worries. As time went on, though, he usually chose the Orpheum Theater, because it had vaudeville acts in addition to films. The theater was beautiful, too, but not quite as elaborate as the Ritz.

At the end of one day when Kitty was working the soup lines, Jonny found her and suggested, "Why don't we go to the Orpheum tonight and see some vaudeville acts? I haven't been there lately."

"That might be fun. I haven't been there in a long time," Kitty replied.

"I'll pick you up at six then," he said. "I thought we could go eat before the show. Isn't there a cafeteria down close to the theater?"

"Great. I'm not sure, but I think you're right. I'll ask Mom where it is."

Jonny arrived at Kitty's house promptly at six o'clock, and they headed downtown. "Mom said that cafeteria is on West 4th Street."

"Is that the one that says 'Hello, Chicken Fry' or something like that?"

"I don't know, but Mom says she'd heard they have good fried chicken."

Sure enough, they both liked the fried chicken at the cafeteria, which they learned was owned by a couple named Nelson and Susan Rogers.

"I think we made a good choice, don't you?" said Kitty as they left.

Jonny nodded in agreement. He liked her company a lot. She was always positive and made him feel important. He could almost forget that he still had unresolved issues back in Michigan and Kentucky. He hardly remembered the hurt he felt over Marilyn's betrayal or the embarrassment he felt at not being able to read well enough to fill out all those forms at work. One day maybe he could overcome some of those problems. But for tonight he'd just enjoy Kitty's company and the vaudeville show.

They were lucky. Jimmy Durante was the vaudeville act that evening. "I love Jimmy Durante," said Kitty, "both on stage and in films. I saw his phantom president film a few months ago. It was really good."

"I heard someone else talking about that movie. What's it about?" asked Jonny.

"I can't remember everything. But basically, it's about a rich man who runs for president, but he isn't a good speaker. They get another guy who looks like him to impersonate him on the campaign trail. There are all sorts of crazy mix-ups in the movie, and it's funny."

"How does Durante fit into it? Is he the presidential candidate?"

"No, no. He is the candidate's friend, who doesn't know about the impersonation because they're trying to keep it out of the press. Anyway, as usual, Durante is funny in the movie."

Chapter 10

Jonny was living a pretty good life. Although many people complained of the storms, especially the dust storms, he realized that Tulsa had it better than those farther west. He continued to help the families he met in the soup lines, as he had all winter. He got to know some of the sad little children, clinging to their mothers as they waited for their bread and soup.

One day when he was off from work, he decided to buy some candy for the kids before he went to the soup lines. He thought it might cheer them up. As he arrived in the hospital parking lot and got out of his car, he noticed the air had a weird feeling to it. He looked across the way and saw billows of dust coming from the west. It was not the first time he'd seen a dust storm coming at the city, but it was worse than he'd seen before. Before he could get to the lines, he saw Kitty coming toward him.

"We need to get these people to safety," she said. "The storm coming up looks bad."

"What do you mean? How can we…?"

Before he could ask the question, Kitty was running toward the people shouting orders for them to follow her into the basement of the hospital. That area quickly became crowded, and people were coughing as the dust began to accumulate. By the time everyone got inside and they closed the doors, it was evident there was a problem with many of the children.

Jonny stepped outside for a moment to see what was happening. The wind was so strong that it almost knocked him off his feet. The lights in the parking lot were on, and those cars entering the area had their headlights on. The parking lot had a weird, ghostly, yellowish look to it.

He remembered talking to a man he worked with who had moved to Tulsa from the Panhandle. The man had said his house was filled with dust all the time out there. His wife had cleaned and cleaned but just couldn't keep the dust out and had wanted to move to Tulsa last year. But this was the first time Jonny had experienced anything this bad since dust storms had not been this severe before. They seemed to be getting progressively worse.

Jonny felt helpless as he stepped back inside, still holding the bags of candy he'd bought. He heard the wailing of two small boys, who looked to be about the ages of his little brothers the last time he saw them.

He turned and knelt down in front of them. "Hey, little ones, it's going to be all right," he said. "Look, I've brought you something."

The children calmed down a little and looked at the small pieces of candy. Suddenly they seemed to have forgotten their fears, and their faces lit up with smiles.

"Thank you so much," their mother said. "Aren't you the young man that brought them shoes last week?" When Jonny nodded, she said, "You're a nice young man. Your mother should be proud of you."

Her words stung as he thought of how he'd failed his own family. Well, he couldn't do anything about that right now, so he just went on over to some other children, trying to do the best he could to bring solace to as many as he could. Both he and Kitty worked the crowd as best they could, him giving out candy and Kitty talking to the parents and relaying words about how the storm was blowing on past. By nightfall, it had calmed down enough that they could get back to where they were staying, but the winds were still blowing, and it still seemed a little unsafe for the young ones to be out in the weather.

When the mothers and children had left, Jonny saw that Kitty had sat down on the steps by the hospital. She looked a little like she might be sick. Maybe she's just had a long day, he thought. He decided to walk over and speak to her.

"Hey, are you okay?" he asked.

"Yes, I suppose so. This dust has really got to me. I had pneumonia as a child, and as the dust storms have gotten worse, my lungs have struggled. But I'm all right. It's just…" She coughed for several seconds before she could go on. "My parents really don't like for me to be out in weather like this, especially when a storm comes up unexpectedly like this one did. But how can one know when it will happen?"

"Come on, let me take you home," said Jonny. "You sure don't need to be out in this wind."

"Thank you. My mom is probably frantic right about now," Kitty said as she walked with him to his car.

When they arrived at her house, Mrs. Stearns was waiting on the porch. Jonny walked up to the house and spoke to her.

"Thank heavens you brought her home," she said. "I was imagining her having to walk in this or who knows what. I don't know how much she's told you about her health, but she does not need to be out in this dust. Her lungs have always been a problem, even when she was little."

"Oh, Mom, it's not that bad. I told him you were probably frantic," she said smiling at Jonny.

"I was frantic all right," she admitted. "So I do appreciate you bringing her home. Will you stay for dinner?"

"No, I'd better go on home now, but thank you for asking me. I will another time."

As he left, he heard Kitty have another coughing spell, and he sensed that she might have been trying to play down her condition a little. Her mother seemed to consider it a serious one.

The next day's storm was even worse, with silt flying through the air. In some areas of town, the wind blew down telephone poles and ripped signs off their posts. The bright electric lights looked dim, and many cars had their headlights on all day. At work, Jonny heard several people talking about feeling like they couldn't breathe. He thought about Kitty. If these people who didn't seem to have any lung problems had trouble breathing, he wondered how she was feeling.

For the next several days Tulsa had really unusual weather. Several times there were both dust storms and severe thunderstorms, including a lot of hail and heavy rain. One heavy dust storm that hit Tulsa blew all the way to the eastern seaboard. Several commercial flights had to be canceled at the Tulsa Municipal Airport because of poor visibility. Every day seemed to bring a new disaster to the area. Jonny continued to work both at East Texas Oil Company and at the hospital, but he did not see Kitty out and about during that time.

As April came in, it seemed that springtime had arrived and things had settled down a little. One day when Jonny wasn't working, he walked up to a little store just four blocks from his apartment. When he came out with his groceries, the sky seemed darker than usual at that time of the afternoon. As he walked, he noticed it kept getting darker. He looked around and saw a black cloud approaching from behind. Soon he felt the wind on his back. It felt like more than just wind. Then he realized it was a gritty substance—dust! Before he got back to his apartment, it had gotten almost completely dark. He almost ran into a man walking down the street.

"What in the world is happening?" the man asked.

"Lately we've been having some bad dust storms like I've heard they have out in the Panhandle area," Jonny said.

"I'm new in town, but I've never seen anything like this. You can feel the dust blowing on you. My shoes are getting dusty!" the man said.

"Yeah, I hope it doesn't start doing this all the time." Jonny walked on, but he too was getting a little fearful.

Chapter 11

Jonny had thought of Kitty several times the last few weeks. She had looked so tired and weary when he had taken her home that evening. He had not seen her out and about since then. But knowing about her health problems, he had not expected to see her.

One evening when he got off work, he decided to stop by and check on her. When he pulled into her driveway, a young man was coming out of her house. He looked at Jonny with a quizzical look on his face. Jonny parked and got out of his car. Before he took a step, the young man spoke to him.

"Hey there! Who are you? And what are you doing here?"

"I just stopped by to see Kitty. Who are you?" Jonny asked.

"I'm Kitty's boyfriend, and I don't like competition," he said with a sneer on his face. Although Jonny had not considered that he and Kitty were a couple in any way, he was a little surprised because he'd never heard her mention having a boyfriend.

He hesitated a moment and then said, "Well, I don't think I'm competition, so I guess you're safe." Although Jonny spoke the truth, he was angered by what the guy said. He stood there a few moments after the guy walked down the street, and then he knocked on Kitty's door.

Mrs. Stearns came to the door and ushered him into the living room, where Kitty was sitting on the couch. She still looked a little pale, but she said she was feeling much better. Jonny could not decide whether to ask about the guy he'd seen leaving or not. They talked a little about the people they'd met in the soup lines, and then Jonny said, "Who was that guy that was leaving when I drove up?"

Kitty rolled her eyes and looked at her mother and then back at Jonny. "Oh, that was Vic. We dated for a while right after I graduated from high school. We were both working at the grocery store. Did he say he was my boyfriend?"

"Yeah, he did," Jonny said. "Is that true?"

"I broke up with him two years ago, but he still comes around once in a while. He just acts like we're still dating, and he's told other people that he's my boyfriend. I don't know why he does that."

Her mother spoke up. "I think he's crazy. I've told Kitty she needs to confront him about telling people he's her boyfriend."

"I kinda feel sorry for him," said Kitty. "He told me one time that I was his only friend. When I broke up with him, I told him that he could still be a friend, but I didn't want us to date anymore."

"But he's just weird," said her mother. "And lately he's been coming by more. I think you need to tell him not to come around anymore."

Jonny listened but did not say much. He didn't know what to advise, but the guy seemed strange to him—even dangerous.

Jonny ended up staying for dinner, and he felt like Kitty's family enjoyed having him there. They reminded him so much of his own family.

When he was ready to leave, he asked Kitty, "Have you gone back to work yet?"

"No, but I plan to this coming Monday. I'm feeling much better." Kitty walked with him to the door. "I'll probably see you next week."

Jonny felt good when he left, but he kept remembering the guy he'd met in her yard–Vic–and worried about Kitty. She hadn't dated the guy in two years, and yet he still considered her his girlfriend. That didn't seem right. She seemed a little vulnerable. He remembered a man back home who was abusive to his wife and children, and Vic reminded him of that man.

The next week, true to her word, Kitty was back at work. Jonny saw her on Saturday as he checked on some of the children he'd gotten to know, and late in the day he actually spoke to her.

"I'm going out close to one of the Hooverville areas to help a family get set up in their little shack this afternoon," she said. "I probably won't see you until next week."

It was late in the afternoon when Jonny left the parking lot of the hospital. After he got home, he decided to go down to a little restaurant on Route 66 to get something to eat. About the time they served his meal, he noticed that it seemed to be getting dark outside. "Is it getting dark already?" he asked the waitress.

"I hadn't noticed. It does seem darker than it did just a bit ago. The radio said something about a storm coming this way. Maybe it's just getting darker because of the rain." She went to the window. "I don't know. The sun's still up, but it looks dark out there too."

"I hope it's not one of those dust storms like we had last month. That was bad!" said one of the other customers.

By the time Jonny left the café, it had become so dark that he put on his headlights. The wind was ferocious, and it looked like there was something black whirling around in front of his car. He drove cautiously, but it became almost impossible to hold the car on the road. Before he got back to his apartment, the traffic had slowed almost to a stop, and he saw some cars that had pulled off the road. The black-looking dust was swirling around, and he could hear the wind whistling outside his car. Even though his windows were rolled up and his doors were closed, he could taste the dust as it infiltrated the car. He was a little afraid that he would not make it home, but was relieved when he saw the driveway.

As soon as he got in his apartment, he remembered that Kitty had gone out to help the family from the soup lines and wondered if she'd made it home before the storm hit. He recalled that she had given him her phone number, but he couldn't remember where he'd put it. After looking in several pockets, tables, and drawers, he found the crumpled piece of paper with the number written on it—or at least he thought that's what it was. He hurriedly dialed the number on the piece of paper. He was thankful when he heard Kitty's mother's voice.

"Hello," she said.

"Mrs. Hearn," he said. "This is Jonny. Did Kitty make it home yet?"

"No, she hasn't. And I'm worried sick. Have you heard from her?"

"No. I just got home, and it's really bad out there. Do you know exactly where she went to help that family?"

"Not really. She said it was in the general area of where the encampment is for the migrants, but it was not in the encampment."

"Okay. I'll go look for her, but if she calls, find out exactly where she is. If I can find a phone, I'll call you again from the area if I can't find her."

"Okay. Thank you so much." Jonny could hear the panic in her voice, and he suspected it meant there was a good chance Kitty was in trouble.

Getting back in his car, he realized that his chances of finding Kitty were not great, but he had to try. He knew a way to get back to the main highway to avoid most of the traffic, which was slowing down every minute. He took the alternate route and was on his way out of town in minutes, but the traffic was almost as bad as on the main road. He thought he knew the general area where Kitty would be, judging by what she'd said.

Just before Jonny reached the encampment, he saw a few little shacks that housed people who planned to stay in Tulsa. As he approached the area, he saw a crowd out in front of one of the shacks. There were pieces of furniture scattered around on the porch. He decided to try asking about Kitty there. When he had parked and started toward the porch, he heard someone say, "I think she needs a doctor."

The crowd parted a little, and he saw Kitty sitting on a chair near the door. She was gasping for breath, and he could tell she was scared.

"I went over there and called an ambulance," another man said as Jonny approached the porch. "They should be here soon. They were over at the encampment."

Jonny walked up to Kitty and asked her if she was okay. Her answer was another spell of coughing and wheezing. It appeared to him that she shouldn't wait for help. He was afraid to offer to take her back in to Tulsa, and more afraid not to.

"I can get her to the hospital as fast as they can," he said as he turned to her. "Can I take you to the hospital?"

Gasping a couple times, she finally nodded her head. "Help me get her to the car," he said to those around them. One of the men picked her up and carried her to the car, and within a few seconds they were on their way to the hospital.

As soon as he turned her over to the nurses and doctors, he asked where there was a phone he could use to call her parents. Her mother picked up on the first ring.

"Mrs. Hearn, I have brought Kitty to the hospital, and she'll be all right. They are taking care of her. Can you come, or do you need me to come and get you?"

"Oh, we can come. We'll be there in a few minutes."

When Kitty's parents got there, Jonny left her in their care. He was relieved and glad he was able to help. Later they told him that, according to the doctors, it was fortunate that he got to her when he did and was able to transport her to the hospital.

She was in the hospital for more than three weeks. Her lungs were filled with dust. It was a common condition during those times, but because she had long-term problems with her lungs, her condition was worse. Jonny checked on her periodically when he worked in the hospital, and called her parents a time or two. He had trouble getting a picture of how she was doing, and since he wasn't family, the doctors would not talk to him.

One day as he was enteringthe hospital for work, he saw Kitty's parents coming out of her room.

"Is she getting better?" he asked her mother.

"I think so," she said. "One day she seems stronger, but the next day she doesn't seem to be doing well at all. She is breathing a little easier, though, so I guess that's a good thing."

Jonny could tell Kitty's mother was worried. He was too. "What does the doctor say?" he asked.

"He seems optimistic now. He said when you first brought her in, he was worried they couldn't save her, but he says she's doing better and showing signs of recovery."

"That sounds good," Jonny said.

"Yes, but it just worries me that I don't see a lot of improvement. I can't tell you enough how much I appreciate your going out there and finding her. I keep thinking if you had not gone looking for her, we might have lost her." She choked up on those last words.

Jonny did not know how to respond. It was a funny thing. He had never been a particularly religious man, but it almost seemed like a surreal experience that evening when he'd decided to go find Kitty. It had seemed like someone was telling him he needed to go out there. He used to hear his mother talk about God "nudging her" to go help someone, and he thought it was funny, but that night he felt the same way. He felt as if someone had been "nudging him" to make that trip out in the bad dust storm to find Kitty. Maybe there was something to his mother's faith after all.

Chapter 12

When Jonny was young, his mother always took him and his siblings to the little Baptist church down the road. As he got older, he resented it. When he left home at age 16 to find work, he felt free to abandon the habit of going to church. Most of his friends did not attend church, and much of the time he was completely exhausted on Sunday after working six days straight.

One Sunday when Jonny had a day off while Kitty lay close to death in the hospital, he decided to go to church, just to see what it was like. He had passed a church on Boston Avenue several times, so he chose to go to it. It was a Presbyterian church. He had no idea what the difference was from the little Baptist church back home, but he decided to give it a try.

He assumed that they might dress up a little on Sundays, judging by the people he'd seen coming out of the church a few weeks ago, so he put on a coat and tie—kind of like he'd seen the Texas Playboys wear on Friday nights. When he entered the church, he realized he was right. Most of the men were dressed in suits with coats and ties. He was welcomed by those who stood at the entrance of the church.

When the service began, they sang a few hymns, most of which Jonny found familiar, but there were one or two new ones. As the preacher began to speak, Jonny's mind began to wander a little. Suddenly his attention was brought back to the moment.

"How long has it been since the Lord spoke to you?" the preacher asked. "John 14:26 says, 'But the Counselor, the Holy Spirit, whom the father will send in my name, will teach you all things and will remind you of all things I have said to you'—that means God speaks to us in many ways."

Jonny sat up and listened. "God speaks in a variety of ways," the preacher went on to say. As he listened to the sermon, Jonny was more and more convinced that God had spoken to him the night he went out to look for Kitty. He didn't speak to him directly, but the preacher affirmed that sometimes God speaks by nudging us in the right direction. Maybe his mother was on to something after all. He would have to apologize to her for thinking she was wrong about God nudging her. Now the preacher had said that it could happen.

"Hey there, young man," someone said as he was about to leave when the service was over. He looked around and saw an older woman behind him. "We're glad you came to visit today," she said.

"Thank you," he responded. He was still thinking about what the preacher had said. "Do you think God speaks to us even today?" he asked before he'd really thought about what he was going to say.

"Oh, yes, I certainly do," she said. "I wouldn't be alive today if my neighbor had not come and found me one time after I'd fallen and hit my head. She said she was asleep on her couch, and suddenly she woke up and just knew she needed to go next door and check on me. I will always believe, as she does, that it was the Lord speaking to her."

Jonny was amazed. It was the first time he'd heard anyone talk about that except his mother. "I was just wondering. My mother used to say that God often nudged her to do something, but I didn't believe her. But lately some things have happened that made me believe she might be right. When the preacher was talking today, it just fit in with my questions."

"Young man, I think you're on the right track, and I hope you'll come and worship with us again soon."

"I certainly will," Jonny assured her.

He left feeling uplifted and yet aware of how selfish and wayward he had been the last few years. He felt he had thought only of himself when he left Michigan, and not of his sister or his mother. He thought of the letter he'd sent to David. Had David actually read it? What did he think? Johnny wondered about his mother and Naomi. Did they really think he was dead? What would they do if they thought so? Had David encouraged Jonny's family to give up and declare him dead? What would it be like to go back where everyone thought he was dead? Would they be glad to learn he was alive, or would they be angry he'd been gone so long with no contact? Maybe he should not have asked David to check about declaring him dead. Maybe he should just never go back. He didn't know. He knew one thing: he needed to start going to church.

After that Sunday, Johnny tried to go back to the Presbyterian church every time he could. He even spoke to the pastor a time or two. He saw the same lady he'd talked to the first time he visited.

Kitty had been in the hospital for more than a month. Although she had made some progress, she was still unable to go home. Her parents were getting impatient with the doctor's reports. One Sunday when Jonny finished work at the hospital, he decided to go visit Kitty again. He had not been able to see her for a couple weeks.

As he entered her room, she appeared to be sleeping, and her face looked pale. For just a moment he feared she might be dead, but then she moved slightly and opened her eyes.

"Hey there, girl! How're you feeling today?" he asked.

"I think I'm feeling a little stronger the last few days," she answered. "It's the first time I can say that, but I really am feeling better."

"I'm so glad to hear that. I was beginning to worry, and I know your parents have been concerned too. I was afraid that dusty old dust was going to get you."

"It just about did, but don't let me fool you. I'm stronger than you think I am," she laughed.

It was the first time he'd heard her laugh since she'd been sick, and it was good to hear.

"Sit down over there. Just throw that stuff off the chair. I think that's some stuff Mama left when she was here."

"Have they said when you can go home?" he asked.

"No, not really. Speaking of going home, I meant to tell you something the other day. I know you've been thinking about going back home to Kentucky. I think you should do it, even if you don't find out about what your wife has done about the marriage or whether you've been declared dead and all that."

"Why?" he grinned. "I thought you liked having me around."

"I do," she said, "but you will never be happy until you resolve the problems you brought here with you."

"What do you mean? I thought I left my problems back there in Michigan."

She sighed. "No, Jonny, it doesn't work that way. Our problems are inside. Once you resolve them inside, it doesn't matter where you go. But if you have unresolved problems, they just tag along with you wherever you go." She looked him in the eyes. "I know you thought Marilyn was your problem, and in a way she was. She did you very wrong, but you have other problems too, and you can't always just leave your problems behind."

"I still don't understand. What do you mean?" said Jonny.

Kitty twisted around in her bed to face him. "Jonny," she said softly, "what do you want out of life?"

"I'm not sure," he said.

"You told me once that the reason you bought shoes for those little kids in the soup lines was because they reminded you of your little brothers, remember?"

"Yeah, I feel bad about them."

"Well, you can't buy enough shoes for strangers to make up for not helping your family. It's wonderful that you want to help little kids here, but it doesn't give any help to the ones you worry about."

"I guess you're right. I'm beginning to understand what you mean."

"Also, you have talked about your sister and leaving her up there in Michigan with a man who is not good to her. You can't make her feel better by the good you do in Oklahoma."

Jonny looked down at the floor, then back up at Kitty. "So you're saying I really brought all my problems with me then, aren't you?"

"Not exactly. I guess I'm just trying to ask you to think about what's important to you and then go after that. In a perfect world, what would you be doing right now? What would your life be like today?"

"Oh, that's pretty easy. I'd have a little more education, a wife and some children, and a job that supported them. That's about all. How does that sound?"

"That sounds fine to me, and you should be able to do that. But just saying it doesn't magically make it happen. You have said several times how you feel bad that you never got an education, but you haven't gone to school here, so you still have that problem. It stays with you until you make a change."

"I guess you're right," he said. "Kitty, do you believe in God?"

"Of course. My parents are both people of faith, and my family has always gone to church. Why?"

"Well, my mother used to take me to church as a kid, and she has always been a woman of faith, but I've never believed much as an adult."

"I believe God wants the best for us, but we have to work with him if we want to have the best in life."

"My mother used to talk about God nudging her to do things, and I never paid much attention to it until recently," Jonny said.

"What happened recently that made you pay attention?" asked Kitty.

"You remember when I came out and found you near the settlement? That night, I had this strange feeling that someone or something was telling me to look for you. Then when you were so sick, the first thing I thought about was what Mom always said about God nudging her to do something. It was really weird."

"I've had those kinds of experiences too," Kitty said. "Anyway, I'm glad something got you out there. I probably wouldn't be here if you had not come."

"I've made a pretty big mess of my life, so I guess it's good that I did one thing right."

"I hope I didn't hurt your feelings by saying you should go back to Kentucky," Kitty said. "I really like having you here, but I don't see any way you can be truly happy until you resolve your problems back home. Maybe then you can return. I don't know what the future holds for you, but going out for entertainment every weekend seems to be postponing the problems and not solving them."

"Thank you, Kitty. You've helped me see my life in a different light. I may just have to take your advice. You're a smart lady."

They visited a few more minutes, and he could tell that Kitty was getting tired again, so he stopped talking, and they just sat in silence for a few minutes. Suddenly the door was pushed open, and a young man walked in. Jonny thought he looked familiar but couldn't place him. Kitty seemed surprised and maybe a little upset at the young man's appearance in her room.

"Victor, what are you doing here? I asked you not to come."

At that point, Victor interrupted her, saying, "And what is he doing here?"

"Victor, please, I tried to explain to you. Can we just talk about this a little?"

She looked at Jonny. "Would you mind giving us a minute? Don't go away, but I just need to try to talk to Victor a few minutes."

Kitty's face looked both angry and sad. Jonny stood and said, "Sure. I'll be outside, and I'll return to say goodbye before I leave." He went out the door reluctantly, but he knew Kitty didn't need two men in her room who refused to leave.

He spoke to a couple of guys who worked at the hospital as he went outside and smoked a cigarette. He had decided to wait until Victor left before going back in, but after nearly 20 minutes, he went back inside and started down the hall toward Kitty's room. Before he could get halfway down the hall, a nurse came running out of her room yelling for help. At the same time, Victor ran out of her room, saying, "I didn't do a thing to her. You're lying." The nurse got help, and they both ran into Kitty's room.

Jonny followed Victor all the way back down to the area where he had gone to smoke earlier. "What happened?" he asked.

"I don't know. She just started gasping for breath, grabbed the bell and rang it, and by that time she was turning blue, and then the nurse came."

"What were you talking about? Why had she told you not to come back to see her?" Jonny asked.

"That's none of your business," Victor said. "You had no business being here in the first place."

"What were you yelling at the nurse about? Was she accusing you of hurting Kitty? Her lungs were not strong, so if she got upset, maybe you caused her to be unable to breathe."

"She was lying. It was not my fault. I have a right to be with her in the hospital. No one can tell me not to come, not even her mother, or even her." He turned to Jonny. "You're the one who should not have been here. You caused her to turn against me."

Jonny looked at Victor. "You may not have meant to hurt her, but if she told you not to come to the hospital, then you should not have come! So even if her problem was not caused by you directly, you shouldn't be here. Do you under-stand that, you idiot? When a person is sick and they tell you not to come around, then you'd better listen." Jonny was so angry at the man that he wanted to sock him in the face.

Victor turned and took a big swing at Jonny, barely missing his nose. Jonny couldn't resist. He swung back hard and fast, and Victor ended up on the floor of the concrete porch, with his head bleeding. He didn't move. Jonny stood there a moment. Was Vic dead? If so, would Jonny be charged with murder? Now was the moment of decision. Should he run away, or should he stay? Suddenly he knew what he had to do. He couldn't run away this time. He turned and ran toward the hospital entrance.

He opened the door and shouted, "Hey, we need help out here!" Seeing a nurse coming toward the door, he went back out to where Victor still lay on the concrete. Within minutes the nurse and an orderly had Victor on a gurney and inside the hospital. As they walked into the hospital, Jonny explained to the nurse that he'd got into a fight with Victor, and he'd knocked him out.

"Hey there… Who are you, and what are you doing here?"

"Oh, I think he'll be okay. We were looking for him because one of the nurses says he upset one of her patients who had breathing problems, and the patient died."

Jonny stopped momentarily as he took in the news about Kitty. He swallowed hard, and felt light-headed for a few seconds. "What was the patient's name who died? Was it Kitty?"

"Yes, I believe so."

Jonny looked around and saw a bench nearby and sat down.

The nurse looked at him. "Are you all right?" she asked.

"Not really," he said. "Kitty is, or was, a friend of mine. Do you know what he did to her?"

"I think he just upset her because he kept hanging around the hospital, and she had told him not to come. Former boyfriend maybe." The nurse left, and Jonny decided to leave too.

For a few days he lived in a fog. How could Kitty be gone? As much as he grieved for his friend, he knew her parents must be feeling much worse. He spoke to them briefly when he attended the simple service for her at a small church near her home. Afterward, he faced the fact that it was probably time for him to get serious about returning to Kentucky.

The next few weeks were difficult. Jonny was torn. He had been in Oklahoma long enough to feel at home there. He had made a few friends and had lots of fun on the weekends going to shows. Before he left, though, he had to make a visit to

Kitty's parents. He owed them that. They had taken him in as if he were their son. He dreaded the visit. He had not seen them since the funeral, and he wondered if they would want to see him at all.

When he pulled into the driveway that evening, the house looked sad. The shutters were drawn, and he could barely see a light on through the door. He sat in the car for a moment, gathering his courage and thinking of what he might say to comfort Kitty's family. He saw that one of her brothers' cars was there, but he wasn't sure which brother it was. He got out of the car and walked up to the door. Before he could knock, the door opened and Kitty's mother stood there looking at him for a moment and then put her arms around him and burst into tears. He held her tightly for a bit. "I'm so sorry, Mrs. Stearns."

She said, "Jonny, Kitty was happier than I'd seen her in a long time when she was around you."

"Kitty was a special person. I don't think I've ever seen anyone who loved people as much as she did. She genuinely cared about those she worked with. I know you are proud to have had a daughter so kind and caring."

Kitty's mother wiped her eyes with her apron. "Yes, she was special. The interesting thing was that she told me the same thing about you—that you cared about people more than anyone she'd known. She said that several times after working at the soup lines down at the hospital."

"I'm honored she thought that. I'm certainly not as good a person as she was, but I am a better person because I knew her. In fact, she gave me some advice that last day that I plan to follow."

"What was that?" Mrs. Stearns asked.

"Well, I don't know how much she told you about me, but I have a lot of things to resolve back in my home state of Kentucky. She said I needed to go back there and resolve them, and I'm planning to follow her suggestion. I just wanted you and Mr. Stearns to know how much I appreciated your friendship and how much I admired Kitty. She made a great impact on me."

They talked for a while, and Kitty's brother joined them in the living room, offering Jonny a piece of cake and some coffee. As soon as he finished his coffee, he told them about his plans for leaving Tulsa and heading back east.

Chapter 13

On a sunny but windy day in April 1936, Jonny got in his car. With little more than he'd brought with him seven years ago, he began driving back to Kentucky in his Model T Ford. His car looked a little more worn, but it ran fine.

The road back was long, and Jonny remembered the uncertainty he'd felt years ago. This time, though, he was more mature, and he had a goal in mind. He wanted to settle down, find the right woman, and have a family. He wanted to be a good father and work hard to support his wife and children. He never wanted his own children to suffer the difficulties he'd seen in the soup lines in Tulsa.

He knew that without an education, it would not be easy, but he had also learned that a man could usually find work if he was willing to do anything, work anywhere, and refuse to give up.

Each day he drove almost all day long. On the first day of his trip, he could see the wide expanse of wheat fields and occasionally a large herd of cattle grazing on the side of the road. Just before dark he found a little motel, and on the second day he found another. As he continued driving, he saw fewer wheat fields and more of the landscape he'd grown up in.

In three days, he made it into Ohio by sundown. He hoped the little store about a mile down the road from his home had a phone by now. It seemed as if most businesses in Tulsa had one. He stopped at a store not long after he crossed into Ohio and asked the operator to check for a listing for the store near his home. He thought if the store had a phone, he might be able to call the next day so his mom would not be too shocked to see him. Unfortunately, the operator said there was no listing for the store near London, Kentucky. He thanked her and the store manager. Before he returned to his car, he asked for directions to the nearest motel in the next town. After he checked in and found a little café nearby, he realized he was ready to rest. He slept soundly and arose early the next morning.

Crossing the line into Kentucky late that morning, Jonny began to feel different. As he drew closer to London, he let himself soak in the feeling and think of the good things about his home, his family, and his friends. By the time he arrived at home, he believed he was ready to see his family. He envisioned his little toddler brothers as they were seven years earlier.

Nothing could have prepared him for the sight that met his eyes when he drove up and got out of his car. He saw a basketball goal by the side of his house and two young boys running around the goal, pushing and shoving and shooting a basketball into the hoop. They were almost as big as Jonny! Who were they? Could they be his brothers?

Suddenly the door burst open, and his mother walked out, looking as if she wanted to be sure this stranger was not going to intrude on her family.

"Mom," he said. There was silence. He waited a few moments as she stared at him. Then she began to sob.

"Jonny," she finally choked out. "I thought you were dead. They said you were dead."

"Who said I was dead?" he asked.

"Everyone... David... He said we should declare you dead, and Marilyn said she needed to get on with her life. David said she wanted to marry again, and she couldn't unless we declared you dead."

Jonny realized the pain his letter to David had caused his mother. He also realized that what he'd wanted had actually been done. He didn't know whether to be sad or happy that it had worked out that way.

"Mom, I don't know about all that, but what matters now is that I am alive, and I'm home."

She reached out her arms then and embraced him and shouted to the ball players. "Boys, here's Jonny. You remember him, don't you? We thought he was dead, but he's not. Here he is. Come and see him!"

The boys laid down the basketball and walked over to speak, seeming a little awkward.

"Boys, we've got a lot of catching up to do," said Jonny. He looked at this mother. "I didn't even know who they were."

Apparently, Jonny's dad had heard all the commotion and came ambling out of the house. He was almost in Jonny's face before he realized who it was. He seemed to take in the whole scene before he spoke.

"Jonny Boy, it's really you! It took me a bit to believe it was you. We thought you were gone forever. I told them we shouldn't declare you dead, but no one listened to me. Your mom was mourning you like you had just dropped dead in front of her."

"Dad, I'm so sorry to have caused you and Mom all this worry."

Jonny's dad reached out and gave him a big hug. "You're home now. That's the important thing."

The boys went back to their basketball game, and Jonny joined them to try his luck at the game. It was a day of celebration, which lasted far into the night.

After a few days, though, his mother seemed to have had time to be a little angry that he'd been gone all that time.

"Why did you leave and not tell me? I'm your mother! You could have written me a letter and told me you were safe," she shouted at him. "No one should treat their mother like that. I've been worried sick, and that business about declaring you dead was the last straw. I actually had to go to bed after we did that. What am I supposed to do now? Declare you resurrected? Tell me that! Now Marilyn has gone on and married someone else. You've made a laughingstock of our whole family."

While Julia was ranting at Jonny, Hobert appeared in the doorway. Although he didn't say much, he seemed to be agreeing with her all the way.

"I don't have an answer, Mom, Dad. All I know is that I just felt like I had to get out of that place and go away. I got in my car and started driving. I drove for days. Finally, I ended up in Tulsa, Oklahoma. I found work in the oil fields and later also at a hospital. But I always wanted to come back home. I know I did wrong, but I hope you'll try to forgive me."

After about a week, Jonny's parents seemed to accept the fact that their son was indeed alive and to rejoice in that. But his mom's attitude that day was repeated with almost every friend and family member he met. He realized no one trusted him very much.

Almost as soon as he returned, Jonny set about trying to find a job. He went over to talk to David, his brother-in-law, to whom he'd written the letter. His sister Sue was perhaps the only person he saw during those first days who did not condemn his actions for leaving and not telling anyone. She just said, "Hallelujah!" when she saw him. He thought it was because David had already told her he was alive, but he learned later that David had kept his confidence and had not told anyone—including his wife—about the letter. When they were alone, David told Jonny that he hadn't told Sue because he was afraid she'd "let it slip" when she was with her sister Naomi, who often came to visit.

"Man, I need to find a job, David," Jonny said while he was there.

"Well, why don't you come up to Blackstar with me and see if they need any help? I've been working up there in the mines for several months."

"Do you really think I could find work up there?"

"I don't know, but it'd be worth a try. You can stay with me in the rooming house this week and check things out. It's pretty good money. Now ... it's hard work, but you're strong, so you can do it."

"Okay, when do you go back?"

"Tomorrow morning early."

"Okay. I'll be over here at whatever time you say,."

At first the two talked about riding together, but then they decided to take both cars in case Jonny had to work in another mine or needed his car to look for a place to stay if he got a job.

Jonny told his mother he would be leaving the next morning to find work at Blackstar. She seemed glad to have her oldest son—and a hard-working one at that—back at home, even if for a short time. Jonny also told her if he did get work, she could count on him bringing most of his check home to her and the kids.

The first day Jonny landed in Blackstar, he went straight to the boss and was hired immediately. He didn't even have to wait a day or so to start work, because one of the miners failed to show up, and they needed help badly. As it turned out, Jonny worked a full week and brought home a good bit of money that week.

He felt good about having worked hard, but he sensed a bit of resentment when he met neighbors and former friends who knew of his disappearance. "Where have you been?" they'd ask. "Have you been in the pen or something?" When he told them he'd been working in Oklahoma for a few years, they seemed to either not believe him or to belittle him for not telling someone where he was.

It didn't feel like home to him, even though his mother appeared to have forgiven him. But most of his other relatives seemed to doubt him and didn't trust him. He did feel comfortable around his two younger brothers, who had been very young the last time he'd seen them. Both were almost in their teens now, and they seemed fascinated by this older brother they barely knew. And his younger sisters, one only a baby when he left, were a little shy around him. He had not seen Naomi or Harris, and he didn't know if he was ready to see them. He wondered about them. He asked his mother, and she seemed evasive.

When they finally came to visit one Sunday afternoon, Naomi seemed too quiet, and Harris stayed in the other room most of the time. Jonny tried to talk to Naomi, but she clammed up and just kept saying she was fine. He wondered what she had told their mother about his disappearance or if she'd said anything at all. He figured if he just waited long enough, he'd find out.

After several weeks of working at Blackstar, Jonny went to David and Sue's for supper one Saturday night. When he got there, he saw they had other company. Sue introduced a man by the name of Thomas and his daughter Ellie, who looked a little younger than Jonny. She was very quiet at first, but seemed very mature.

"And that young man over there is Lonnie," said David, pointing to a young boy who looked and acted different. He did not respond to David but sat on the couch ignoring what was going on in the room.

Ellie was very short and had dark brown, almost black, hair like her father. When Sue had introduced the family, she had not mentioned anything about the young lady's mother, so Jonny wondered where she was. He didn't ask, though.

As they talked, Sue asked Ellie how they were doing, and Ellie replied, "We are fine, and I really appreciate all your help last year when Mom died. Lonnie had a hard time understanding it, but he's doing better now."

"I'm so sorry about your mother," Jonny told Ellie.

"She had been sick for two or three years before she died. It wasn't a shock or anything, but it's been hard on me in many ways."

"Ellie is the woman of the house these days," said her dad. "The hardest thing for both of us, I guess, has been taking care of Lonnie."

There was something about the petite woman that was interesting. When she spoke, she had a gentle voice. She was patient with her younger brother. He didn't talk much, and Jonny could not always understand what he said, but Ellie did. She never raised her voice or seemed annoyed, although her dad sometimes did. During their visit, Sue and Ellie spent most of the time in the kitchen talking, putting the food on the table, and cleaning up after supper. Afterwards they brought out coffee and cookies.

"And where did you say you'd been living the last few years?" Thomas asked Jonny at one point while they were there. "David said something about they thought you were dead or something."

David interrupted. "Yeah, he was gone so long, we thought he'd died. But as you can see, he's alive and well, and he's working with me in Blackstar now."

It was as if David was trying to convince Thomas that Jonny was a good guy or something. Jonny was puzzled, but there was one thing for sure: Thomas was not convinced. He looked and sounded a little wary of Jonny.

When Jonny prepared to leave, David suggested, "We'll have to do this again."

Jonny agreed but was not so sure about Thomas and Ellie—especially Thomas, who remained silent. Ellie was polite, but she said little in response to David's suggestion that they might get together again.

CHAPTER 14

David proved to be a good friend. He not only welcomed Jonny as a co-worker, but he also had welcomed him into his home and tried to help him get back into the community and family. They had not had many conversations about Jonny's letter, though.

One day, Jonny offered an apology. "I'm sorry about writing you that letter and telling you not to tell anyone. I know that made it difficult for you."

"Yeah, boy, you put me in a terrible situation. I didn't want to tell anyone because I was afraid they might talk about it to the wrong person. Like I said earlier, I didn't even tell Sue until after you were back home. Boy, was she ever mad at me for not telling her!"

"I'm sorry to put you in that predicament, but I didn't know what else to do. After I learned what could be done legally, I could not think of anything else. And then I met the guy who was visiting his father in the hospital, and when he told me that he was going back home to Georgia, I just thought it was my chance to send a letter. And you were the only person I felt sure I could trust."

"I really appreciate the trust you put in me. I knew Sue wouldn't mean to betray a confidence, but you know how she is. She might say something to her mom before she thought about it."

Jonny agreed. "By the way, how is Naomi doing? She seems so busy with the kids and all. I haven't had a chance to talk to her alone."

"I don't know, Jonny. I worry about her sometimes, but Sue insists that she's okay. You know she and Harris came back to Kentucky just a few weeks after you left, and she was pregnant with Susie. Harris had lost his job, and I really thought Naomi was going through a difficult time. But then she and your mom started sewing for people, and she seemed happier. I don't think she and Harris get along that well, but who could get along with him?" David laughed a little.

Jonny was quiet for a bit. "I wonder why she ever married that guy anyway." He had decided not to talk about the past in Michigan, especially since he had not talked with Naomi about it. He wasn't even sure she knew what had happened.

"Me too," said David. "Did she ever tell you he cheated on her?"

"No, but I'm sure he did," Jonny said. "He's just kind of what I call a creepy person."

Jonny dropped the subject after that. It would do no good to stir in that nasty pot, but he did want to talk to Naomi. He wanted to see if she and Harris had moved on from the incident with Marilyn or if he was still like he was before Jonny left.

Chapter 15

Naomi couldn't believe it when she first heard Jonny was back home. It wasn't that she had ever believed he was dead, even when they'd convinced her mother and dad that they should declare him dead. She just couldn't believe he had returned to Kentucky. On the one hand, having her brother home was so exciting; on the other, she had changed a lot over the last few years, and she knew that Jonny probably had too. As she thought about him being back home, she remembered the day he had left. At the time it seemed like everyone had deserted her, including her big brother.

The last time Naomi had seen Jonny, Harris was late getting home that night, and she had become worried. She walked toward Jonny and Marilyn's apartment building, thinking they would know why Harris was late. Before she reached the steps to the entrance, however, the door burst open and Jonny came rushing out of the building. When he saw her, he came down the steps before he spoke to her.

"Harris hasn't got home yet," she said. "Do you or Marilyn happen to know where…?"

"Don't go in there…" he almost shouted at her.

"What…?" she began again.

"I said for you to stay out of there," he said. "You don't want to go in there."

"Okay, but where is Harris?"

"Naomi, I can't talk right now. I'm too angry. Just go on back home, please."

"Okay. I will."

Naomi always wished she had insisted on more information, but she hadn't. There was only one explanation as far as she was concerned. When she discovered that Jonny had left, it confirmed her conclusion, but she just had to move forward in a daze.

Because she and Harris had moved back to Kentucky about a month after Jonny had left Michigan, she had just tucked the whole thing in the back of her mind and moved on. When she realized that she was definitely expecting her first child, it pushed her thoughts about that evening further back in the crevices, and she had little time to think about it.

Naomi had tried to forget about Marilyn, too. Then, two years ago she'd learned that Marilyn had moved back to Kentucky and was living with her parents. At first, Naomi had panicked. What if she ran into Marilyn somewhere, or what if she came looking for Harris? However, after a month or so, she had again not allowed herself to think about it.

But two months ago, when the subject of Jonny had come up again, she heard that Marilyn had insisted on his parents declaring him legally dead. Apparently, she had found a new boyfriend and wanted to remarry but could not do so as long as she was married to Jonny. She begged Julia and Hobert to declare Jonny dead, which they eventually did. Naomi had insisted to her parents that he was not dead, but they had ignored her advice. Initially, her dad had listened and seemed to doubt that they should declare him dead. Her mother, however, had bowed to the wishes of Marilyn and the others. Now Jonny was back, resurrected.

The night they had seen Jonny for the first time after he returned, Harris made some snide remark about him, saying he couldn't believe Jonny had left his family like that and expected all of them to forgive him for deserting them in a time when the economy was so bad. "They should disown him," Harris insisted, "instead of welcoming him like he was the prodigal son or something."

"No!" Naomi shouted.

"What do you mean, 'no'?" Harris fired back.

"I mean you are not to talk about Jonny like that!"

"Oh, the little lady is mad, is she? Are you threatening me? What will you do if I do talk about him again? Huh? Spank me? Leave me?"

"You'd just better keep your mouth shut about Jonny."

Naomi felt her face becoming hot and flushed. She didn't ever remember being this angry, even seven years ago when it became clear to her that Harris had cheated on her. She was still young and idealistic back then. She thought she could save her marriage, that Harris would change. Now, however, she knew the ugly truth. It was true that they had stayed together, but their relationship had not improved.

Naomi started to stomp off to the kitchen, but Harris stopped her. He grabbed her around the waist and encircled her with his arms. "You know you can't do without me, little lady. Who would buy you clothes or other things little ladies love?"

"Turn me loose, please. I just want to be left alone."

She twisted out of his reach and headed for the kitchen. He laughed. She hated it when he did that. There was no real love left between them, yet she stayed with him. In one sense he was right. She could not imagine trying to live on her own. The couple had moved to their own place about six months after they had returned to Kentucky. Harris was glad for it, although they had only moved a few houses down the road from his wife's parents.

A lot had happened since Jonny had left over seven years ago. Naomi remembered the way she felt when she knew she was going to have a baby, one that was conceived before she knew about Harris' betrayal. With two little ones, how would she live? She couldn't expect her mother to take care of her and the children too. Her mother was still raising her own children. She didn't need grandchildren to raise too.

Continuing to think about that night, Naomi recalled that before she had got to the kitchen, she heard one of the kids awaking from a nap. Her anger had ceased as she headed back to their room to welcome them back into her presence. They had saved her the last few years, even as they had worn her out. Having two small children who adored her had made it possible to ignore the hurt and pain of knowing her husband was often unfaithful.

The next day Naomi had taken them to see their grandmother. Julia was in the yard when they arrived. Susie and Bobby ran to her as soon as they saw her. She grabbed them and hugged them tightly.

"Naomi, are you all right?" her mother inquired when she saw her.

"Yes, I'm just a little tired today, but I'm okay."

"You look upset. Is everything all right at home?"

"Yes, you know Harris. I just get weary with him sometimes. He was saying stuff about Jonny, and I got really mad."

"Why? What was he saying about Jonny?"

"He was saying Jonny was bad because he left, and you and Dad didn't know where he was. It's none of his business. He never does anything for you all, and he's been around all the time."

Although Naomi could tell her mother was sympathetic, she didn't say anything one way or another. She simply commented, "I thought Jonny and Harris acted rather strange toward each other the night you all were here. Did you notice that?"

"I don't know. They are just very different people. Jonny is a hard worker, and I think maybe Harris is jealous. You know what he said? He said you and Dad should disown Jonny because he stayed away so long that you had to declare him dead. I got really mad when he said that, and I yelled at him about it."

"Honey, you know we couldn't ever disown any of our children. That's just ridiculous! Just don't even listen to him about that." Her mother patted her shoulder. "We love all of you too much to disown any of you."

"I know, but it still made me mad when he said that."

"Naomi, have you told me all you know about Jonny's leaving? I have always thought there is something you have never told me about the reason he left. Even back when you first came home, I thought there was something you were not telling me."

Naomi walked a few steps away from Julia. She had always thought she could not reveal the whole story, but maybe the truth should come out. "Yeah, Mother, I do know more. But I could not tell you at the time, and I don't know if I can tell you now either." She sat down on the steps and began to cry.

Julia walked to the side of the porch and told the boys to watch Susie and Bobby, and then she came over and sat beside Naomi and asked, "Can you tell me if I promise not to say anything?"

"It was the person Marilyn was cheating on Jonny with. It was Harris." She continued to sob, but finally looked up and said, "Was it right for me to stay with Harris? I ask myself that question often, especially now that Jonny is back. I wonder if I should have run away, like Jonny. Or maybe I should have divorced Harris. I don't know."

Julia kept her promise and did not say anything or ask any questions, but at least Naomi felt better after getting the truth out in the open. Maybe it would help to be able to discuss things in the future. It was especially true now that Jonny was back home. It just felt right to Naomi that her mother know the whole story, even though there was nothing she could do about it. She knew it would help explain a lot of things. And, in the case that she decided to leave Harris, her mother would probably understand more about why she did it. Of course, it seemed that most people did not accept a divorced woman, no matter what the reason for the divorce. Women were just supposed to take whatever the man wanted to do and not pay any attention to it. It didn't seem fair to Naomi.

Naomi and Julia had been able to do fairly good business making clothes for people in the neighborhood. Harris had acted better in the last couple years, even though he occasionally left Naomi in the evenings for a while. She had her suspicions about where he'd gone. She noticed he was a little more careful about saying things about what women could or could not do. She suspected it was because she had proven she could make a little money by working just as he could. The changes over the last couple years may have been the reason she'd been able to stand up to him when he'd said those things about Jonny.

CHAPTER 16

After her talk with her mother, Naomi kept thinking more and more about the possibility of leaving Harris. He was not dedicated to their marriage. Why should she have to stay with a man who cheated on her and cared nothing about their relationship? Maybe she should talk to Jonny about it. He would understand because he knew all about what Harris had done, and he also knew how people felt about a divorced woman. But how could she talk to him alone? She had not really had a chance to do that since he returned.

Fortunately, the next day Jonny dropped by to see Naomi and her kids. As soon as he entered the house, she ran and hugged him, and then she broke down in tears. He just stood there with his arms around her for a few moments and then said, "Hey, it's all right. Tell me what's the matter."

"For one thing, I've missed you so much, Jonny. You have no idea how I've missed you."

"I thought about you a lot, too, Naomi. I know I did you wrong, just leaving like I did. I did you and Mom both wrong. I worry about that a lot. I know I can't go back and correct it, but is there anything I can do for you now? That's what I came to ask you."

"I just want to talk to you. The night I was looking for Harris and you came running out of your apartment building, I understood what had happened, although you didn't say it. And then when you left, I was so mad because I felt like you were the lucky one. I kept asking why you didn't take me with you. But in a way I understood."

"I am so sorry, Naomi. I don't know how I can ever make it up to you."

"It's okay. You did what you had to do, and I'm not mad at you now."

Jonny looked at her. "Did you ever confront Harris?"

"No, I didn't. I often acted mad, though, and I think he suspected that I knew. He just acted like it'd never happened, and I felt like I couldn't leave, because what would a single woman do? When I expressed anger at Harris, he would just act like a woman couldn't get along without her man."

Jonny hung his head. "I'm still so angry at him, not so much for myself but for the way he's treated you."

"During the next few days after you left, I had to do something to keep myself busy, so I started using my sewing machine that Sue had given me when we got married. After a few weeks, Harris lost his job. I'm sure you were the reason they hired him in the first place. After he lost his job, we soon moved back to Kentucky. By then I knew I was going to have Susie, so I was glad to be back at home."

"That must have been hard on you. Did you tell Mom anything?"

"No, not then. I think she knew something was going on between Harris and me. But I did tell her the other day—since you came back."

"How did she react?"

"Well, she could tell I was hesitant to tell her, so she promised not to say anything, and she didn't."

"Has she had any contact with Marilyn?"

"I don't think so, but I'm not sure. Not long after we moved back, Mom and I decided to continue sewing and making clothes for people. Oddly enough, we're doing pretty well with our little business."

"Oh, that's great. We have a working woman in our family!"

"I never allowed myself to think about what Harris had done to me, and the few times when I'd lash out at him, he'd just laugh at me and act like I couldn't do without him. And as you know, we have two little ones now."

"I'm not sure where you're going with all this."

"Well, I guess I'm just now thinking about what I should have thought about when you left. Do I want to live all my life with a husband who cheats on me?"

"Naomi, I don't know what to tell you. I'm afraid you'll have to make that decision by yourself. But I will say that things are changing where women are concerned."

"What do you mean?"

"Well, first of all, women are finding ways to support themselves. Just like you are learning how to sew and make a little money, lots of women are finding that they can work to support themselves the same way men can."

"I never thought about that, although I have recently asked myself if I could sew enough to make a living at it. I don't know."

"Another thing is, while it's true divorce is still frowned upon, people seem to have realized that sometimes it may be necessary." He grinned. "Even the Bible says adultery is reason enough. But the main thing is, you have a right to be happy and live with someone who's a friend and a companion to you—the same way I do."

When Jonny left, even though he had not told Naomi what to do, he had made her feel he would not forsake her if she decided she could not live with Harris anymore. She would have to think about her situation some more. Maybe her husband would change. Of course, she had said that for most of their marriage, especially after they had returned to Kentucky and had babies. She needed him to change and be home more. He was pretty good with the kids when he was there. In fact, he was better than she had imagined he'd be. Maybe they would make him a better person. Maybe he would be faithful to her for the sake of the children. She hoped so, but how long should she wait for him to change?

Chapter 17

One evening Jonny's mother asked him why he appeared to be sad. He responded with "I don't know, Mom. I just feel like such a failure. I've wasted seven years, and I still have no better jobs or opportunities than I did years ago. I really don't like working in the mines, but I don't know what else to do."

"What would you like to do?" she asked.

Julia was a kind woman. Short and pudgy, she had a great sense of humor. Jonny was a lot like her in temperament. He would fly off the handle easily, but he was also kind and gentle and generous with people.

"While I was in Tulsa, I realized if I had a little more education, I could be a supervisor of some kind. When I was given an opportunity to supervise, I failed because I couldn't read well enough to fill out the forms needed to give reports."

"Why don't you go back to school? The younger boys are going to school. You could go too."

"I don't know. They'd be embarrassed if I went back at this age."

"Maybe, but you'd still learn something, even if they were embarrassed."

"But I'm almost 30 years old."

Julia sat for a moment, looking at her oldest son. "I think I heard they had some kind of night school for adults. Why don't you ask about that? Maybe you could go to school at night and work during the day."

"That might be worth a try."

Jonny felt better after talking with his mother, even though he wasn't sure if he could work and go back to school at the same time. He was just about to step out of the room when there was a knock at the door. Julia went to the door, and to their surprise it was Marilyn's parents. Jonny didn't know what to do. He couldn't just disappear, and he had no idea what to say.

Julia stood and looked around a few seconds and then said, "Why, hello, Mr. and Mrs. Moore. Come on in."

No one said anything for a bit, and then Mrs. Moore said, "Jonny, we heard you were back in town. I guess we can just say that it's good you aren't dead."

Jonny looked at them a few moments. Mrs. Moore looked older. He imagined that whatever Marilyn had said and done since he left had aged her. Finally, he said. "Mrs. Moore, I know that running away like I did was probably not the best thing to do."

Mrs. Moore looked at him, a hint of sympathy in her eyes. "And Tom and I both know that what she did was not the best thing either."

"Well, it's all long behind us now, and there's no way to change it," Jonny said.

"That's the reason we came over today, just to say that we're sorry the way things happened. Tom and I feel that maybe part of the problem was that the marriage was more our idea than it was yours and Marilyn's."

Julia joined in the conversation. "Hobert and I have said the same thing. Parents may want the best for their children, but the decision of who to marry can't rest with the parents. We never should've interfered in that."

"At the time," added Mrs. Moore, "I was convinced that you two would be perfect for one another, but how did I know? I hardly knew my own child, let alone Jonny."

Julia spoke again. "I think it was true of all of us. We got this idea that the two of them would be good for each other, but none of us really knew what these two young people wanted."

Jonny looked at Mrs. Moore. "So, are you saying you forgive me for running off like that?"

"Absolutely. You had a right to leave Marilyn. She did a terrible thing to you. But again, sometimes people don't know what to do when they're in an unhappy situation, so they do the wrong thing. She's never talked much about her feelings, except to admit she was wrong."

"I learned when I came back that she had remarried, after they had given up on finding me alive. I guess that was the best thing, but I should have come back sooner so people wouldn't have thought I was dead."

"About a year ago she met a man who seemed to make her happy, and six months later they married. I hope it's the right one for her, but what I have to realize is that people make mistakes, just as we all do. And it had to be her decision, no matter what I think."

After the Moores left, Julia looked at Jonny. "I didn't realize you felt badly about leaving Michigan. I guess I just always thought you believed you did the right thing."

"Oh, no, I had a lot of guilt about the way I handled it, especially because I had to stop sending you and the family any money. You know, by the time I left that year, I had been helping you all for several years."

"Yeah, and I always felt bad about that. I told your dad, after I thought you were dead, that I would never forgive myself for not letting you go to school."

"Like I said earlier, I do need to get more education, but I am actually glad I was able to work and help when I was young. While I was in Tulsa, I learned a lot, and I think I am more mature now. Maybe I can go forward in a better way now."

"That reminds me of a question I've been wanting to ask," remarked Julia. "What made you decide to return? From what you've told me, you had a pretty good life in Tulsa."

"For a while I thought I'd just stay there, but I kept thinking about you and the kids and Dad and Naomi—especially Naomi. I knew she only agreed to come to Michigan because of me. It got so I thought about all that a lot."

"Was there something that made you leave there when you did?"

He thought a moment. "Have I mentioned a girl named Kitty to you?"

"Not that I remember…Was that a girlfriend in Tulsa?"

"Not exactly, but Kitty Stearns was a young lady I met in Tulsa." Jonny went on to tell his mother a little about Kitty's work with the Salvation Army, their friendship, and meeting her parents. "She had the idealism and optimism of youth and the wisdom and strength of an older generation," he added.

"So, she told you to come back home?" Julia asked.

"No, but she helped me see that the things I struggled with there were because of things that happened here. She actually said the problems were inside me, but that I would have to come home to resolve them."

"Kitty sounds like a bright lady. Will you stay in touch with her?" asked his mother.

"No, I can't, but she had a great impact on my life." Jonny looked down, not knowing how to explain what happened.

"So, why won't you stay in touch with her?"

"She died a few weeks before I left Tulsa," he responded. He went on to explain what had happened.

"It sounds like you learned a lot while you were there and that you are a better person because of it," said his mother.

"Truer words were never spoken," Jonny confirmed. "I did learn a lot from Kitty and her parents. The thing is, they were a lot like you and Dad."

Chapter 18

On Saturday, Jonny stopped by David and Sue's house for a visit. While he was there, Thomas Webb and his daughter stopped by also. David took Thomas out to the barn to show him his new mule, while Jonny was left to visit with Ellie.

Jonny, never having any trouble thinking of something to say, commented, "Well, it's just you and me now. Tell me what you've been doing."

"Mostly just cooking, cleaning, washing, and a little gardening," she said with a smile.

In moments they were chatting away with no restraints. It was odd how they seemed to feel right at home with one another so quickly. At some point Jonny asked, "Do you know anything about some adult education classes where I could go back to school and learn to read and write a little better? I'm at a real disadvantage with only a third-grade education."

"I don't know, but a teacher who used to live with us when I was in school lives just about a mile from me. I'll ask her if she knows."

"That would be great. I'd appreciate your asking her."

Ellie looked at him. "You know, she might even be willing to teach you if there are no classes available. If she doesn't know about any classes, I'll ask her if she might consider tutoring you. Do you have anything specific you'd like to do or be trained to do once you've got a little more education?"

"Not really. But I've learned that without being able to read well, I can't move up in anything. I tried one time in the oil fields to be a supervisor. My boss was really helpful, but obviously he couldn't make me able to read well enough to fill out all those papers."

Except for Kitty, Ellie was the first person Johnny had met that he could be himself with. There is something about people who let you know they will help you if they can, even without having to say it. Ellie was like that. He left there feeling a bit encouraged.

The next week, David told Jonny that Ellie had some information for him regarding school and that after work on Friday he would have Ellie come over for a visit so they could talk. True to his word, when Jonny arrived on Friday, David had invited Ellie to come too.

While Sue was making dinner for them, Ellie sat down across from Jonny and began talking. "You remember the teacher I told you about?" Jonny nodded. "Her name is Miss Mattie Arthur. I asked her about the adult schooling, and she said there is some but not in Laurel County. She said she hopes there will be in a few years. Meanwhile, though, she said she would be glad to meet with you and see if she might be able to help you."

"Really? You are a wonder. Thank you so much! When can I meet with her?"

"Well, you are at work all week, and she teaches school, so I told her I'd see if you could come over next Saturday. Would that be possible for you?"

"Yeah, I could come, but I don't know where she lives. I know about where you live. Could I come to your house, and you take me over and introduce me to her?"

"I could do that, as far as I know," she agreed.

"You just don't know what this means to me," Jonny said appreciatively. "I've been hoping for something like this for almost all my adult life."

After dinner Jonny stayed a while, and so did Ellie.

"Where's your dad tonight?" Jonny asked her.

She hesitated a bit before answering. "He said he had work to do. And speaking of work, I'd better get on home because I've got some things left to do there too."

After she left, David said, "Jonny, you know that lots of folks around here don't trust you much, don't you?"

Jonny looked at him. "I hadn't thought much about it. Why? What have I done around here to make people not trust me?"

"Well, that's just the point. You haven't been around here for a long time, and while you were gone, no one had any idea where you were or what you were doing. Some folks are suspicious of that kind of behavior."

"Well, I can't help what..."

"Now wait a minute, Jonny. I'm not saying they shouldn't trust you. But I know you well, and I know some of the reasons you left, but not everyone knows any of that. The reason I'm telling you this is that Thomas is not happy that you seem to like his daughter. We can see where this might be heading, and Thomas is just fearful—that's all. I thought you ought to know before you go over there. I'm not saying you're doing anything wrong. I'm just telling you how Ellie's dad sees it."

"Okay, I do like her, but I doubt she has an interest in me. I'm probably not the type of person she'd think was right for her. But I do appreciate her helping me find that teacher."

David sighed. "Ellie's a good young lady, kind and all that. But I think Thomas probably would have a problem with anyone who took her away. How would he manage without her? Ever since his wife died, Ellie has just been there— cooking, cleaning, and doing what most wives would do. Even before that, she was doing most of the housework because her mother was sick for two or three years. Especially during the last year, Ellie had to do everything."

"Yeah, I hadn't thought about that. What happened to her mother?"

"She had stomach cancer. It was really bad, I understand."

"How long ago did that happen?"

"She died last spring. I'm not sure when she got so sick that she was bedridden, but I know it was a long time."

After their talk, Jonny wasn't too sure if he should go over to Ellie's the next weekend, but he decided to go on and face whatever he had to. By the next Saturday he was ready to go meet the teacher, but he still dreaded going to Ellie's and wondered if he should have asked for directions to the teacher's house. He realized that perhaps his asking Ellie to take him to meet the teacher had more to do with wanting to see Ellie again than it did with his not knowing how to get to the teacher's house.

Jonny had promised to get to Ellie's by 10 o'clock in the morning, and he was right on time. Maybe that would make Thomas feel better about him. When he got out of his car, he saw that Thomas was in the yard cutting wood. He was a slight man of average height. His hair was jet black, and he reminded Jonny of the many Creek Indians he'd met in Oklahoma. He always wore overalls and looked very neat. He barely acknowledged Jonny when he spoke, but Jonny walked over to where he was working and asked him how he was doing.

"I'm doing fine. If you're looking for Ellie, she's in the house."

"She told me she knows a teacher down the road who might help me learn to read better. She promised to take me to meet the teacher today. Will that be a problem for you if she does that? If it is, I could get her to just give me directions."

"No, that's okay. Go on in and get her to go with you."

Jonny suspected Ellie might have already won the argument about her going with him. Whatever the case, he went up to the door and knocked. Ellie came to the door with her sweater on and her purse in her hand, ready to go.

"I'll be back in a while," she said to her dad. "I've prepared some sandwiches for lunch, so we can eat when I come back."

"Okay, I'll try to get this wood chopped while you're gone," he said.

As they approached the modest home of the teacher, Ellie walked ahead and knocked on her door. When the door opened, a lady appeared with a big smile. "Hello, Ellie… And you must be Jonny," she said.

"Yes," responded Ellie. "And Jonny, this is Miss Mattie Arthur."

Jonny liked Miss Mattie instantly. She was a little older than he, but still an attractive lady who seemed to have a lot of knowledge and patience. She was dressed as a professional, like some of the teachers he had seen at the church in Tulsa. Her hair was dark brown and wavy but not curly. She was taller than most of the women he knew, but she didn't look too tall. It just added to her professional appearance.

As soon as they entered her living room, Jonny saw that Miss Mattie had already been working to get ready for him. She had some testing materials she could use to determine where Jonny was in his reading ability, and she seemed to know exactly what he needed.

"Ellie, it will take me a few minutes to work with Jonny and determine his reading level. Go on in the kitchen and pour yourself some coffee while we work. It won't take long." Ellie quickly did as Miss Mattie requested.

Once she determined his reading level, the teacher began to ask Jonny what he wanted her to do. She seemed to want him to tell her what kind of schedule they would establish.

"What were you thinking you needed to do in terms of meeting with me? Would you be able to come over every other week on Saturday?"

"I think I could do that if you could see me every two weeks. Maybe you could give me work to do at home, and then I could come every other week, and you could check up on me. You could just tell me what I'd need to do."

"Yes, I could give you material to read and study, and then when I meet with you, I could check your reading ability again and see what you've learned."

"How much would it cost me?"

"I've been thinking about that, and I wondered if you'd consider working for me a couple hours each time after we finish the lesson. I live alone, and I'm finding it hard to keep my place looking good. The lawn and that field out there get so grown up that I'm ashamed of the place. I also have a little garden out back, and there's always something that needs to be done out there. Would you be willing to just stay and work a while after each lesson?"

"Yeah, I'd be glad to do that. Of course, you'll have to tell me what you need done each time, but that would work fine for me."

By the time Jonny and Ellie left, he had an armload of books and some pages with questions written on them to answer. He felt good about Miss Mattie.

"I hope I haven't got you into more than you wanted to do," Ellie said on the way back to her house.

"No, you certainly haven't. I like that teacher. I think she can help me a lot. I just hope I can do the work."

"She taught me for four years until I graduated from eighth grade," Ellie said. "I always liked her. I wish I could have been like her. Like you, I wish I could have got more education, but that just wasn't possible."

When they arrived back at her house, Ellie invited Jonny to have a sandwich with her and her dad, and he accepted. It was somewhat awkward with her dad, but he was polite.

"Now, where have you been for the last several years?" he asked.

"I spent the last seven years in Oklahoma," Jonny replied. "Tulsa."

"I've heard that's a rowdy town—lots of bars and criminals."

"Yes sir, that's right, but there's lots of other stuff too. Have you ever heard of Bob Wills?"

"I've heard him on the radio a few times."

"I went to see him perform live several times. Tulsa also has lots of movie theaters and other places with good shows."

"I hear that those places have lots of dancing and drinking too."

"Yeah, they have that too," Jonny said. He could tell Ellie's dad was not impressed with what he'd heard about Tulsa, so he decided to drop the subject.

"I didn't have a lot of time for entertainment, of course. I was working all the time, mostly in the oil business, but I worked some at one of the hospitals and once for the Tulsa Ice Company. You know, it was hard times out there too, just like here."

"Sounds like you changed jobs a lot..." Thomas stood and announced, "I've got to get down to the garden now."

It didn't seem likely that Jonny was going to make a favorable impression on Ellie's dad, so he stood also, and looking at Ellie, said, "Thank you so much for introducing me to the teacher. I think I can learn a lot with her help."

Jonny was anxious to get started on all those things the teacher had told him to do. She had given him several "easy readers," as she called them, and told him to practice reading them aloud as well as silently. She had also given him some questions after each story and asked him to write down his answers for them. In addition, there were several flashcards with more difficult words on them. Jonny was supposed to learn the words and definitions—10 each time—printed on the backs of the cards.

Jonny's schoolwork was keeping him busy, but he enjoyed it. On weekends when he was home, he would often show his work to Ellie, who was a good teacher herself. She would encourage him to read the little books aloud to her when they were alone.

One night when he was reading one of the books to her, Thomas came in the room and asked, "What are you doing?"

"I'm practicing my reading," answered Jonny. "This little book is about farming."

"You've probably never done any farming much," challenged Thomas.

"Well, I guess I haven't, but I'm learning some things. When I was a young kid I helped my dad, but that's been a while ago. This book is talking about crop rotation, which I'd heard about," said Jonny. "They talked about that in Oklahoma. The government is trying to get farmers to practice rotating crops to prevent topsoil from blowing away. I don't think many of them are buying into it, though."

"I've never heard of such a thing. What does that mean?"

"They say that if you plant the same thing over and over, like they have the wheat for example, it ruins the topsoil and causes it to run down, and then when the soil is no good, it just blows away when these storms come through. I don't understand too much about it, because, like you say, I haven't done much farming."

Chapter 19

The teacher had been so much help to Jonny, and eventually he began to think that soon he would be able to do some work he'd been unable to do in Tulsa. He looked for opportunities in the mines to read any forms or materials that were available. He wanted to be sure he could read well enough before he applied for any job that would require him to read. One reason he liked the schoolwork was that it gave him opportunities to see Ellie every other week. She had been very helpful to him, but he was always careful not to spend too much time at her house. She often met him at David and Sue's on the weekends when he was invited to visit them. Since they knew the way Thomas felt about Jonny, he believed Sue may have tried to make sure the two were not there at the same time.

Much of the conversation between Jonny and Ellie was about his studies. He would usually bring his books and questions with him when he went to his sister's house, hoping Ellie might be there too. When they were together, they could forget that her dad did not approve of her seeing him.

One day Jonny said to Ellie, "What grade did you say you finished in school?"

"I went through eighth grade," she told him.

"I wish I could do that."

"Well, you can, I think. Miss Mattie could teach you to that level. I don't know if she could get you through high school, though."

"I need to see what her plans are, and then I can decide what to do."

The next month the teacher said she'd like to retest Jonny to see how much progress he'd made. "I think you're doing so well that I may not have to teach you too much longer."

"What are you thinking I can do after that? Will I be able to get some kind of certification when I reach a certain level?"

"The problem is that even if you're reading at a certain level, like eighth grade, you still couldn't get a certificate for finishing eighth grade without studying math and science and other subjects. You see, the certification comes from studying all the subjects. But it will still help you to learn to read at the eighth-grade level, even if you don't have an eighth-grade certificate."

"What would I have to do to get the eighth-grade certification?"

"You'd have to study all the other subjects they teach in the first eight grades, and then you could take a test for the certification," Miss Mattie explained.

"I probably need to think about doing that, but now I need to finish my work on reading," Jonny said. As he left that day, he continued to think about the possibility of getting his eighth-grade certification.

The coal-mining work was just as it had been a few years ago—hard, back-breaking work. One day Jonny and David were loading a car and were nearly finished. It had taken them about an hour, and they were ready for a break. Suddenly they heard the familiar "Fire in the hole! Fire in the hole!" As always, Jonny had a feeling of fear that someone might get hurt. They often did right after the guy blasted out some more coal. The week before, an unsteady section had fallen on a man and covered him up before anyone could rescue him. He left a wife and three little kids. Jonny didn't mind the work, but he kept thinking there ought to be a better way to live.

A few weeks later Miss Mattie scheduled Jonny's test to determine his level of reading. The day of the test, he was a little nervous.

"What if I'm still not reading at the level I need to be?" he asked Ellie one night when he was working with her at David and Sue's.

"But you're farther along than you were," she assured him, "so you can just keep working on it."

"You're right," he agreed. "I have decided that I want to start working on the other subjects, too, because I want to at least get that eighth-grade education—like you have."

"Will Miss Mattie be able to help you with that?"

"I'm not sure, but she probably would be able to tell me how to do it, or who could teach me." Jonny sat back in his chair. "What was the hardest subject you had in school?" he asked Ellie.

"I'm not sure. I don't remember any of the subjects being too hard," she answered.

The next time he had a lesson with Miss Mattie, she told him he had scored at the eighth-grade level in reading.

"Now I want to become an eighth-grade graduate," he said. She seemed pleased with his decision. "How can I do that?" he asked her.

"Well, since you're an adult, you'll just be studying to become proficient in the subjects you'd normally study in school, but you wouldn't actually be attending classes. So, the first thing we'd do would be to give you the test for eighth-grade graduation and see how you do. Then we could decide what you need to study. My guess is you already know a lot of the stuff just because of your age and experience."

"Can you do that, or will I need to go somewhere else to get the test?"

"I can get the test at school and give it to you. When it comes to studying some of the subjects, I may have to refer you to someone else, but we'll just wait and see."

"Thank you so much," Jonny said gratefully. "I never thought I'd get this far."

In the following weeks, he took one step at a time as he was tested, obtained some study materials, and began his journey to receive a little more education. He and Ellie spent almost every weekend working on his lessons. She was very helpful. Although most of the time they studied at David and Sue's, sometimes they went to her house. On those occasions, Jonny felt the tension between himself and Thomas. It was not usually combative, but Jonny knew Ellie's dad didn't approve of him spending so much time with his daughter.

On one of those nights, as Ellie walked him out to his car, Jonny asked her if she'd consider marrying him.

"Of course I'd consider it," she said. "But you know what the problem is."

As they talked, it was obvious Ellie wanted to marry Jonny, but she was hesitant about talking to her dad about it. Jonny knew how she felt. From what she told him, Thomas had practically set his foot down about that issue.

"Well, just think about it. We'll work it out some way," Jonny promised as he left that night.

A few weeks later on a Saturday when he and Ellie were at David and Sue's, he said, "Let's just go talk to him about it, Ellie. All he can do is say no."

"Okay. Do you want to come over tomorrow afternoon then?"

"Yeah, I can do that. I'll need to leave by four o'clock to go back to Lynch, but I'll be there by two."

Jonny was nervous but also excited to finally get an answer. Ellie was an adult, of course, so she didn't really have to have her dad's permission, but the couple would certainly like to have his blessing. They had decided it would be better to begin by letting Jonny talk to Thomas by himself, and then she would come in after the discussion had started.

When Jonny arrived, Ellie was in the kitchen cleaning up after lunch, and Thomas came to the door. He invited Jonny in but did not look happy to see him.

After a short discussion about the weather, Jonny said, "Thomas, I've come to talk to you about something I've been wanting to say. Ellie and I have been seeing each other for several months now, and I would like your blessing to marry her."

Thomas shifted uneasily in his chair, giving the impression that he was not ready to bless Jonny in any way, especially to marry his daughter. He didn't say anything right away, though.

"I know Ellie is very valuable to you and it'd be hard on you not to have her here," said Jonny. "I want you to know she and I would always help you in any way we could."

At that, Thomas seemed to become indignant with Jonny. "I'm not thinking of myself, young man! I'm thinking about what's good for my daughter. Ellie has never been around a lot of men, especially men who have been on the wild side. She can be easily taken in. She doesn't know that you could just up and leave her like you did your other wife."

"Dad, that's just not fair," said Ellie from the door. "Jonny had good reason to leave Marilyn. She was cheating on him."

Thomas looked at Jonny and frowned. "See, that's what I mean. She's just believing whatever you tell her. She doesn't know where you've been the last seven years, and there's no one to say that what you've told her is right or wrong."

"Don't treat me like a child, Dad. I may not have gone out with a lot of what you call 'wild' men, but I'm 24 years old, and I think I've learned a few things about people. Also, you trust David, don't you? He knows the story of what happened when Jonny was married to Marilyn. I think his sister Naomi knows about it, too, and she was up there in Michigan when Jonny left."

"Well, they are family, so I know they believe him, but neither David nor Naomi ever saw what happened out there in Texas or Oklahoma or wherever he was all those years. I've read about those oil workers in Tulsa. They are a despicable bunch of rowdies—roughnecks, they call them."

The conversation seemed to be going nowhere. Finally, Jonny said he'd best be going back to Lynch. Ellie was almost in tears as she walked him back to his car. Jonny felt it would not help for him to spend much more time there. "I'm sorry, Honey," he said, "but you know I'm not giving up. I'll see you next weekend."

"Oh, I think there's one other thing bothering my dad about me getting married. Before Mom died, she was worried about who would take care of Lonnie after she was gone. I promised her I would always take care of him. I know I can't just assume you would help me with him. So, I guess you need to think about that before you make a commitment to me."

"Aw…, I had sort of guessed you would be responsible for him. I would want to help you with him. We could take him in whenever we need to."

Ellie turned and hugged him tightly and said, "Thank you so much. I just wasn't sure any man would want to do that."

"Listen, don't you worry your little head about that. And if the subject comes up with your dad, tell him Lonnie will always be welcome in our home and can come live with us if he needs to."

Ellie thanked Jonny again and headed back to the house as he left.

The next weekend when they met together at David's, they decided that getting her dad's approval was probably not going to happen.

"Could we just not tell him?" asked Jonny.

"That's probably what we'll have to do," said Ellie. "I don't think he'd ever approve. He won't even listen to anything about us getting married. I tried to talk to him about it last week, and he got mad."

"He wouldn't hurt you, would he?" Jonny asked.

"Oh, no, he'd never do anything like that. He'd just tell me not to, and I can't seem to hold my ground in any kind of argument with him."

"Well, let me think about it, and maybe we can come up with a plan to get married without telling him. When we do tell him, we'll already be married, and there's nothing he can do about it. Of course, he might not want me around, so I don't know how we'd come to visit."

Chapter 20

Knowing that Thomas would not approve of him marrying Ellie and that he might in fact try to stop her, Jonny had decided to ask Ellie to meet him in London one Friday in March. He was half afraid she would not do it. She had seemed to want to elope when they had discussed it, but he knew her dad was deadset against them marrying. He had not trusted Jonny from the beginning, and of course he really needed Ellie at home. Jonny could understand that in some ways, but was it right to expect her not to want her own family?

Jonny knew it was a difficult time for Ellie. She loved her father, but she also wanted to marry and establish her own family. She had expressed this to him several times. Jonny hated to make it more difficult for her, but she didn't seem to blame him at all. Finally, he had an idea. He'd just drive over to her house one weekend, pick her up, and they'd get married. He was tired of waiting. He sat down and wrote her a letter.

Hello, Honey:

I sure was pleased to hear from my sweetie day before yesterday and that you are o.k., and still quilting on my new quilt. I would like to see you right now for I could love you to death—but I wouldn't want to do that, would I? Say honey, I can't hardly stay away from you. It's the hardest job I ever had—that is stay away from you. I said I'd be back to see you in two weeks, and that will be Sunday. Hope you will be at home and will be glad to see me. Guess I'll work Saturday night and come home Sunday morning. So if you can just be at home Sunday evening I can come over—if it's not snowing like it was last Sunday. I worked here all week last week and didn't feel good. Say honey, there's no one I ever longed for as much as I do you and I want you to believe me and I'll always be good to you, little sweetie. Don't you never think I'd get tired of you. That would be impossible, for you are so good and sweet and it worries me cause I can't be with you all the time. I want to talk to you this weekend about an idea I have for us to get married soon.

Bye, bye from the one that will always love you best.

Jonny

On Sunday, February 21, 1937, the sun was shining brightly. As Jonny drove toward Laurel County that morning, he felt better than he had for the last week or so. He had a plan for getting the love of his life to marry him. He knew it would be difficult for Ellie to leave her dad alone. Because of that, he wanted to make sure she agreed with his plan. He would go to his parents' house first and then go by David and Sue's before he went to visit Ellie that evening. He might let David and Sue know of his plans at some point, if Ellie agreed to them. He decided, however, not to say anything to his parents.

When Jonny arrived at Ellie's house, she informed him that her dad was not at home. He had taken her brother over to their neighbor's house, who lived about a mile down the road from them. It was not uncommon for Thomas to be gone when Jonny visited. Her dad obviously had no desire to get to know Jonny better. He had his mind made up about that.

Knowing they might not be alone the whole time, Jonny thought it best to bring up the subject of marriage soon after he came. "Are you still willing to marry me?" he asked.

"Of course. I don't know how we can do it, though. Do you have an idea of when or how we can meet and have a ceremony?" Ellie seemed distressed.

"I thought maybe I could take a Friday off, drive down here, pick you up, and we could get married and then drive on to Lynch. I was thinking David might help me decide where we might get married. He might know someone who would perform the ceremony. That's as far as I've got with thinking about it, except I wish we could do it sometime in March—maybe the 19th, if that suits you. I'd have to give notice in advance about being off from work a little."

Ellie listened to every word Jonny said, and he could tell she was excited about the prospect of going with him. "That sounds good. I like that plan. Just let me know what David says."

When they saw Lonnie and Thomas coming down the road, Jonny could tell Ellie began to get a little apprehensive by the way she was biting her lip. She kept looking up the road toward them instead of looking at him. Before they got within hearing distance, he tried to reassure her that it would all work out, but he knew she hated to go against her father's wishes. At least they now had a plan, and it made Jonny happy. He left soon after Thomas came back, feeling that his being there only made things more difficult for Ellie.

The next few weeks, Jonny and Ellie wrote back and forth every few days. He could tell she was getting a little nervous about the whole thing. He realized her anxiety was partially because she had hardly been out of Laurel County. It would be a big change for her. His letters to her were often meant to assure her that he really wanted her to be in Lynch with him.

Hello Sweetheart,

I received your sweet letter last night and as always pleased to hear from you again. I just got up a while ago. I had to work late this morning. I sure was tired too, but I almost came driving down to see you today. I wish now I was there. I'm sure I wouldn't be so blue. I know I would enjoy myself like I always do when I am with my little girl. Honey, I don't know whether I can stay away from you much longer or not. It's the hardest thing I ever tried. I don't think you'll be any trouble to me at all. When you're here I'll have somebody to talk to and help me cook. (Ha) You cook and me wash the dishes (ha). Say, my cookies I was telling you about—well that's the hottest thing out, hot on the inside and cold on the outside—never saw anything like it! Can't cook cakes or anything. I can't even bake potatoes—think I'll just stick to grilling them. I have a lot of fun cooking and writing to you about it.

I work and sleep and get up and work again. But I get a kick out of life when I know I've got somebody that I love. I've never done this in my life, but I feel better all the time. I don't know why, but I'd do anything for you and always will if you will let me. I don't trust anybody else. I'd give anything if you were with me today. I'd have you spoiled so bad that anybody would hate you but me. And I wouldn't leave either.

The radio is on next door and they are singing church songs. And it makes me want to cry. It's sure lonesome here this evening. But it won't be when you're here with me. I've worked twelve nights straight except Sunday night and haven't felt good either. But I'm feeling better now.

You wrote me about the roads. But I will be down there any way. I might just carry you out of there. I think I could easy enough. I don't think I can wait all summer you know. Besides I might lose you since you got that permanent. Are you any sweeter since you got it? Don't see how you could be, but you might. Now if I was with you every day, I'd mess up your hair and that way I'd see you mad, wouldn't I? I hope nobody else is while I'm away from you but guess not.

Well, Sweetheart, I am wondering what you're doing this blue day. I slept all day yesterday and most all night last night. I'm expecting a letter from you tomorrow as long as my arm. (ha). Sure would like to be with you today but can't, and it gives me the blues. Well, honey, I guess you're getting tired of reading such a long letter. I'll close with love to my little girl as ever, the one that don't forget you,

Jonny

A few days after he mailed the letter, he woke up wondering if it was possible he'd get a letter back that day or the next. He doubted it. He tried to remember which day he'd mailed the letter and whether she'd actually had time to receive it and respond. One way or another, it was all set, and Jonny was feeling better about the possibilities for things working out for him and Ellie. He decided to write another letter to her anyway, because he had not answered her last letter since it had come the day he'd mailed his last one.

Dearest Sweetheart,

I sure was pleased to hear from you as that's the only thing I care about. I've been feeling bad the last couple of weeks, but I am a little better than last week. Just had a bad cold and can't get over it. I've worked every night so far. Don't want to lose any. Just went down to the office and ordered a load of coal so I can keep warm. Oh, boy, it's so cold here and snowing something awful this morning. Sure looks bad. Just looks like the high mountains you read about in stories. It's just one snowstorm after another. Sure hope it don't last.

Let me know if there is anything you need me to get for you before the 19th. I can pick it up here at the company store.

Say sweetheart you said you was afraid something would happen to one of us. Well, honey, let's not let anything happen if we can help it. That's all I care about anymore. It's being with you. I get blue sometimes to hear from you and can't hardly stay here without you. If something happens to you, I might live a long time, but life wouldn't mean anything to me any more. As long as I'm pleasing you, I'm satisfied and I'm not worrying about anybody else or what they say. You said you were already giving me orders. Honey, I'll take as good care of myself as I can, but I've got to work. I need you to give me orders all the time. Wish you were here so you wouldn't have to write them (Ha). But I really don't believe you would be hard enough on me. Do you? If I was with you a while, I don't think I would need very many orders. I don't know whether I'll come down Sunday week or not. Of course, if I don't, that's a long time to stay away from you, Sweetie. Well darling, I'd better close.

I think maybe the bus station in London would be a good place to meet on the 19th, since you'll be riding the bus in from the Colony. I'm wondering about the weather, if it might get so bad the roads would not be passable. What do you think? What will we do? I worry about that. Let me know what you think.

Bye, bye from the one that will love you always,

Jonny

A few days after he wrote that letter, Jonny received a letter from Ellie responding to his offer to get some things at the store.

R.F.D. 2 Box 83
London, Ky.

Dearest One,

Will write you a few lines this morning in answer to your letter received yesterday. Sure pleased to hear from my little man again. Hope this finds you o.k. Leaves me kind of blue. It sure looks gloomy this morning. It's raining and turning cool, may turn to snow here. I just don't know what would be best to do. I'm afraid the roads are going to be bad from the way it looks this morning. Of course, it may be pretty by then, but as you said, we can't hardly depend on it. You asked if I could meet you in London. I couldn't hardly do that, because the bus only makes three trips a day now and it goes up real early about seven in the morning and don't go up any more until one in the afternoon and I'd hate to walk all the way to London (ha).

If you wanted to come in your car and meet me at Dees Store about 10 or 10:30, I could do that or just whatever time you could be there. Of course, I couldn't get there any earlier than 10. The worst I hate about meeting somewhere that way is that something might happen and one of us couldn't be there. Of course, if it was bad raining or snowing you would know I couldn't be there. If we do that, I want you to get there first for I wouldn't know what on earth to do if I got there and you were not there. Everyone would know I wasn't waiting on the bus that time of day (Ha).

If we do that, I'll go up the Moore Ridge. So write back at once and let me know what you think of this plan and if you think it's alright. You can tell me what time you can be there and all about it. I'll try to be there any time you say. Or if you don't want to do this, we'll just have to put it off a while longer.

If you come and it's bad until I can't get out there, will you come on down or what will we do? Write and tell me.

Honey, I'm crazy to see you again, and if things work out as I am planning, I'll be with you this time next month. Well, I must stop and get to ironing. You must answer real soon and tell me what to do. Oh, I don't think of any thing I need except some gloves.

With love, I'm always yours,
Ellie

P.S. I'm looking for a letter from you today, but don't guess I'll get one (Ha).

When Jonny finished reading Ellie's letter, he felt much better. She really did want to meet him and run off and get married! He was excited and believed their plan would work. He would just have to figure out how to get all the paperwork done. He'd need to talk to David about what he'd need to do. He immediately sat down and wrote back to Ellie.

Dear Ellie,

Of course, I would not want you to walk all the way to London. I didn't think to check the bus schedule. I could just come out close to your house—you know that bend in the road right before you get to the teacher's house—between your house and hers? There's a little wide place in the road. Why don't I just meet you there at around 10:15. That way you won't have to walk far at all, no matter what the weather is. I wish I had thought of doing that anyway. That way you won't have to worry about people wondering what you were waiting for (ha). Your dad still won't see me, and it will be easier for you, my little girl. You asked about me bringing you some gloves. I can certainly do that. Just one thing though. What size do you wear? I got you something last week. I didn't think you would get to go to town. I thought it would be too bad. It's been pretty cold up here, but it looks like a warm day today, but I haven't been out since I came home from work.

So I'll see you around 10:15 on Friday at the bend in the road. I can't wait for us to be together all the time, my sweetheart.

Yours Always,
Jonny

After work the next day, Jonny told David to wait a minute because he needed to ask him something.

"Okay, what can I help you with?" asked David.

"Ellie and I are planning to get married," replied Jonny.

"Congratulations, man! Can I come to the wedding?"

"Well, I don't know about that. I don't even know where we'll get married. Actually, we plan to slip off and get married. Thomas is deadset against it, and we just decided he'd probably get used to it if we went on and got married. We plan to leave on Friday morning, March 19. What I am not sure about is where we can get married, maybe on the way back up here to Lynch."

"Let me see," said David. "I think Barbourville would be the best place. I know a preacher up there. His name is Joe Grant, and he would probably come and do the ceremony for you. I'll see if I can find him on my way home this weekend."

"Could you? That would be good. Do you think he could find someone to be our witnesses?"

"Oh, I'm sure he could. I'll mention that to him. He probably has to do that all the time."

From then on, Jonny was convinced that he was a man with many blessings. Things were working out for him and Ellie. He'd be a married man soon. He couldn't believe how much things had changed for him since he'd left Tulsa less than a year ago.

The following Monday he asked David if he had talked to the Grant fellow.

"I did, and he is willing to perform the wedding. He said he could probably find some witnesses too. But you know, Sue and I would like to be there, if that would be all right."

"That would be perfect if you all could come. I think Ellie would like that too. I'll let it be a surprise, though, just in case anything should happen to prevent you from coming."

The following weekend was the week before Jonny and Ellie were planning to get married, and they were both a little nervous. On Saturday when Jonny went to meet with Miss Mattie, he felt a little guilty when he went by and talked to Thomas a few minutes. Thomas seemed a little distant and didn't say much, so Jonny didn't stay long.

When he had returned home from living in Tulsa, Jonny had known he would eventually run into Marilyn, because he knew she lived in the area. When he left Ellie's that Saturday, he stopped at a store in London to pick up some groceries and saw Marilyn walking down the aisle toward him. He hesitated for a moment and then said, "Hey there, Marilyn." She stopped and looked at him for a few seconds.

"I heard you were back in town," she said. "How are you?"

"I'm fine. And you?" Jonny suddenly remembered the hurt and anger he'd felt the night he'd caught her and another man in bed together. Now it seemed as if it had happened to someone else. He remembered how he'd felt then, but he could not feel it now. He realized that after all the years, even though she was still a beautiful young woman, he couldn't feel anything for her anymore. It was just like he was meeting an acquaintance he barely knew. He had to think a few moments before he answered. "I'm doing fine now too. I heard you remarried after you…"

"Yeah, after I heard you were dead. But you're not, of course. I'm sorry I made such a mess of things."

"Well, life goes on, I guess, and we become different people. We can both just go on with our lives. See you around."

Jonny turned around and continued his shopping. Maybe it was all for the best. He wondered now how he could have married Marilyn in the first place. He felt no connection with her and could remember no good times with her. He realized that even before he knew she was cheating on him, she was very different from him in most ways.

He remembered times when he'd talk to her about his concerns for his mother and his siblings. She would always act like he should just forget about them. How could he do that? Her own parents had wanted them to marry, just as his did, but she had never seemed to connect with them much either. She was critical of her mother and seemed glad to be rid of them when she and Jonny moved to Michigan.

He, on the other hand, had worried constantly about his family. Once, when he sent a check to his mother, Marilyn got mad and said they needed the money themselves. He tried to convince her that he needed to do it because his dad was out of a job and his mother needed the money worse than they did.

"Well, he should just get a job!" Marilyn had shouted at him.

When he looked back to the events leading up to his leaving, Jonny realized their breakup was inevitable and he should have suspected something was going on. But he didn't. He remembered his shock when he learned what was going on.

When Jonny met Ellie, he realized she was totally different from Marilyn. Now he couldn't wait for March 19 to come. He planned to wake up before daylight that morning and head down to Laurel County. David was going to leave Thursday evening after work so he and Sue could have time to get ready the next morning. They had both received permission to be away from work on Friday. Jonny knew Ellie would like having David and Sue at the wedding, and it would be a good surprise for her. It was fortunate David had known a preacher in Barbourville who was willing to perform the ceremony.

Jonny remembered his first wedding, which had been performed at Marilyn's house. Both of them had been too young to know the importance of what they were doing, but her parents had wanted her to marry him, and his parents had thought marrying and having a family would "settle him down." At that time he too had thought it would be good for him, but he had never felt about Marilyn the way he felt about Ellie.

On Thursday night before she was to meet Jonny at the bend in the road, Ellie wrote her dad a letter, which she planned to leave on the table the next morning. Thomas had said he was going to work in the barn a while the next morning and then go down to the pasture where there was a fence that needed mending. He had said he would be gone until around noon or a little after.

Dearest Dad,

By now you are probably wondering where I am. Me and Jonny have left to get married this morning. I know you did not want me to marry Jonny, but we love each other, and I believe we will be happy. I hope you will forgive me. I understand how you feel, but I had to make my own decision about this. We want to be able to come back for a visit in a few weeks if you will let us. Sometime in the next week or so, if you will let David know if we are welcome to come for a weekend, we will do so. Also, please know that Lonnie will always be welcome to stay with us at any time.

Ellie

On Friday morning, Ellie had everything planned out. After she prepared breakfast for her dad, Lonnie, and herself, she quickly cleaned up the kitchen as usual and went back to her room as soon as her dad went to the barn to care for the animals. Lonnie had also headed down to the barn soon after her dad had left the house. He liked to think he was helping, although he seldom did anything. Ellie already had her suitcase packed, so it was not long before she was ready to head down the road to meet Jonny. She picked up her bag in one hand and the letter to her dad in the other.

As she walked into the kitchen one last time, Ellie was looking for the best place to leave the letter. She decided to place it in the center of the table where the sugar bowl and the salt and pepper shakers were. She hesitated a moment, wondering if Lonnie might pick it up, but then she decided he would not. He might not even come back to the house until her dad returned. Even if he did, he probably wouldn't go into the kitchen.

On his early Friday morning drive to Laurel County, Jonny had time to think about what he wanted out of his marriage to Ellie. He knew this marriage would be different from his first. He remembered all the hours he and Ellie had spent talking about their beliefs and concerns. He realized he was old enough now to know what he wanted.

Jonny wanted to be a responsible husband and father and a good provider. Even though he would probably never have a lot of education, he was glad he'd been able to learn enough, with the help of the teacher, to read much better. He wanted to be generous to his family and to those in his community. Ellie had said she wanted to start going to church somewhere, and he had agreed they needed to do that before they had children.

Before Jonny realized it, he was headed west on Highway 80, and soon he was on the road toward Ellie's house. When he got to the bend in the road just past Miss Mattie's house, he saw Ellie standing there in her pretty blue coat and dress.

He pulled over, got out of the car, and practically ran to put his arms around her. He escorted her to the car and opened the door for her. Then he placed her bag in the back of the Model T Ford and turned around and headed back out.

They drove in silence for a few minutes and then began their talk as they usually did. He realized their elopement made her a little sad; she felt she might be doing something to hurt her dad. He asked her if she really wanted to do this, and she said yes.

When they got to Barbourville, Jonny knew exactly where to go for their ceremony, but first they stopped at the Knox County court clerk's office, where they met a man named Abe Fedders and were issued a marriage license. Then they went to a room where they met Joe Grant, the pastor who would marry them. Jonny took all the papers to sign.

"Don't we have to have witnesses?" Ellie asked after they had met the pastor.

Reverend Grant looked at Jonny. "Yes, we do," he said, "and I believe they're already here. I'll step out into the hall and see where they are."

"I hate to have some strangers be our witnesses. I guess we should have asked some of our family to come, but I knew Dad would not come, and I just didn't know of anyone else." She looked like she might cry. Jonny walked around and put his arm around her, just as the door opened and in walked David and Sue. "Oh! Oh! I don't know what to say. I am so glad you're here," Ellie exclaimed, running over to hug them both.

"We wouldn't have missed it!" Sue cried. "When David told me of your plans, we both agreed we should be here."

Reverend Grant then gave everyone instructions about where to stand and how he would conduct the service. In a short while, Jonny and Ellie were husband and wife. After paying the minister a small fee and making sure he had all he needed for the marriage certificate, Jonny suggested they get something to eat before leaving. The minister had other plans, but David and Sue agreed, so the four of them walked down to a small restaurant in town and ate lunch. As soon as they finished lunch, David and Sue left to return to London, and Jonny and Ellie drove back to Lynch to spend their first days together. As much as it made Jonny happy to take a new wife, he also felt a bit of regret when they reached the pitiful-looking mining camp he lived in.

"I wish I had a better place to live," he said to his bride. "I'll try for that soon."

"Oh, this is fine. I'm just happy we can be together."

"Me too, but one of these days, we'll have something better. I promise."

"I know, Honey. We will."

Their first week together was hectic, but the two of them were happier than they'd ever been. Ellie was busy getting settled in and learning how to prepare meals each day while Jonny was at work. The couple had little time for her to get to know anyone in the mining camp, but they knew as spring came on, they'd have more daylight in the evenings.

On Sunday afternoon the next weekend, Ellie seemed upset. "What's wrong?" Jonny asked.

"I think Dad may have talked to David by now about us running off and getting married. What time do you think David will get back tonight?"

"I don't know. He just said he'd probably come back tonight instead of tomorrow morning because he has to be at work so early. Do you want me to walk over there and see if he's back?"

"No, we can wait a while. I'm just anxious to know if he's talked to Dad."

When it was late and almost dark, Ellie asked, "Do you think David might be back by now?"

"He might," answered Jonny. "I'll go see."

When he headed out the door, Ellie stood in the doorway for a few minutes and watched as he walked down the street. David did not live far from Jonny and Ellie. Before long, Ellie heard a noise at the front door, and by the time she got to the door, both Jonny and David were coming inside. Ellie couldn't wait to learn if David had seen her dad.

"Did you talk to Dad?" she asked as soon as they were inside.

"As a matter of fact, I did."

"Is he still really mad at me?"

"No, not that I could tell. To be honest, I think he was a little embarrassed because of the way he'd acted about you and Jonny," said David. He went on to say that Thomas had been apologetic and had said to tell both Ellie and Jonny he certainly wanted them to come for a visit as soon as they could.

The couple looked at each other and gave a sigh of relief. David had brought good news to them both.

"I thought he'd be okay with it once we got married," said Ellie. "I just didn't know how long it would take him to accept it."

Chapter 21

On one of his and Ellie's trips home, Jonny talked to Miss Mattie about needing to arrange a way to continue his education in Lynch, because he wouldn't be coming home as often now that he and Ellie were married. "How can I do that? Do you know anyone who might continue teaching me?"

"No, I don't, but I'll ask next week at school or go by the office of education and inquire if anyone there can give us the name of someone to contact."

"Okay, I appreciate your help. I'll see you next time I'm down this way."

One day Jonny said to Ellie, "You know what I'd like to do? I'd like to learn to weld. I think I could do that, and welders make pretty good money. If I could get my eighth-grade certification, I might be able to get a welder's certificate and work somewhere other than the mines."

"That would be great," Ellie said. "I think you can do that. The mines are so dangerous. I worry about you every day."

By summer, Jonny had learned there was a teacher in Lynch who used to teach at the school where many of the miners' children attended but was now teaching adult classes for miners at night and on weekends. The teacher, Mr. Orr, had served in the military during World War I and had been injured. He had some trouble walking, and generally used a cane. His little classroom was in the back of the company store where he worked. Apparently not many people even knew he was teaching adults at night. The first time Jonny met him, he had come into the store for some bread, and he asked one of the other men if they knew anyone who might teach him. Mr. Orr presented himself and told Jonny to come see him the next morning. Upon arrival, Jonny saw that the little room in the back had actually been made into a school room. He had noticed that there was a room there but had not looked inside. Most of the time the door had been shut. When Jonny walked in that day, Mr. Orr was sitting at a desk in front of a few student desks. On the left side of the room sat a little bookshelf with a few books on it.

"What can I help you with?" asked Mr. Orr.

"I just want to go to school," Jonny told him. "I got a lady down in Laurel County to teach me reading skills, but she said I couldn't really be a graduate from the eighth grade until I studied some other subjects, like math and science. Is that right?"

"You're right. Reading is just one thing that makes you educated. You'll need more than that. But the good thing is that if you are reading at the eighth-grade level, it will help you with the other subjects too."

"What subjects do you teach? Do you teach math, science, social studies—those kinds of subjects?"

"Well, I teach whatever you want to learn—if I know it," he laughed. "If I don't, I can probably find a book about it, and I can help you learn from it."

"Can you then give me a test after I study with you and certify that I graduated from eighth grade?"

"Yeah, I can do that. Now, I just teach Monday through Thursday every week. The times vary, but generally we start when the miners get off work, and I work individually with them for an hour or so, depending on what they need."

"That's fine with me. How do I sign up?"

"Just sign your name here, and then I'll look for you beginning Monday."

Jonny couldn't wait to tell Ellie his good news. "You won't believe who I met today!" he exclaimed when he got home that evening.

"Who?" she asked.

"A man named Mr. Orr, who will teach me the things I need to know to be an eighth-grade graduate."

"Oh, that is wonderful. How did you meet him?"

"He works at the store, but he's also a teacher. He used to teach at the schools here in Lynch, but after the war his injuries caused him to have trouble getting around. I don't know the whole story, but now he works part-time over at the company store. There is a little room in the back where he teaches adults in the evenings Monday through Thursday."

Before long, Jonny was making good progress toward his goal of getting an eighth-grade certificate. The next time he and Ellie went back to Laurel County, they went to Miss Mattie's house to tell her about it.

"That's great news," she said. "How long will it take you to do it?"

"Mr. Orr says that based on my scores, I should be able to finish eighth grade by next year. He said I have a great advantage by having good reading skills. He said most of his students had a lot of trouble because they couldn't read well."

"I can understand that."

"I can too, because so much of my trouble before was that I couldn't read well. I could usually figure the other stuff out okay."

"Do you have a plan for what you might want to do once you get the certification?"

"I'm not sure, but one thing I'd like to do is get my welder's license. I don't think I can do that in Lynch, though, so I may have to go somewhere else to do that."

One evening in summer 1939, Jonny noticed that Ellie was especially happy. After they ate, she told him she had some news for him.

"What is it?" he asked.

"We are going to have a little one in our family," she said with a smile.

"Ellie, that is wonderful, just what we need. How long have you known?"

"I've suspected it for a while, but a few days ago when I visited Sue and talked with her, what she said made me pretty sure that I am really going to have a baby."

"You know how I love children, so that makes me very happy."

Over the following months, as Ellie began to gain some weight and look like a little mother, both she and Jonny were excited. Neither of them was prepared for the events of the cold January night the baby was born, however. They had decided that when it got close to time for the baby, they would go down to Laurel County and she would stay at her dad's until after the baby's birth and a week or so afterward so she'd have some help. One weekend when they were in Laurel County, Sue helped Ellie find a midwife, who agreed to come when she was needed.

Jonny and Ellie left Lynch on a Friday night after Jonny finished work. Ellie felt sure the baby would come during the weekend while Jonny was still there. Sure enough, on Saturday morning she told Jonny she was feeling some pains, but since it was her first, she had been told the labor would probably be long.

Jonny worried a little about how Thomas would react to him, because they'd spent very little time together since he and Ellie had married. He was pleased, however, that Thomas seemed happy that they'd decided to come spend some time for this special event. On Saturday morning he seemed to go out of his way to make Jonny feel at home.

The midwife came early in the evening, after Ellie had been in labor for several hours. She instructed Jonny in preparations for the birth, and Ellie had all the little garments needed for the baby laid out on the bed. Jonny had asked Sue and David to come over and keep them company that evening. When it was time for the baby to come, Sue went into the room with the midwife, and David stayed out on the porch with Jonny.

"Seems like it's taking a long time," David said to Jonny after a while.

"You think everything's all right?" asked Jonny.

"Probably. I guess I'm just thinking about our last one, which is our third. You forget what that first one's like after a while."

Time dragged on for a while until finally the midwife appeared through the door, looking worn out and sad. "I'm sorry, Jonny," she said. "After all that hard labor, the baby didn't make it."

"What? I don't understand. What happened? Is Ellie all right?" Jonny stood and started toward the door.

"Yes, Ellie is fine, but wait just a bit before you go in. Sue is helping Ellie get cleaned up a little first. I am so sorry. The cord was wrapped around the baby boy's neck, and you know there was just nothing we could do."

The midwife checked back in with Ellie and Sue and then left, assuring them she would return the next morning to help with preparing to bury the tiny baby.

Jonny was bewildered as he waited for Sue to tell him he could go in and be with Ellie. How could they not have a baby after all Ellie had gone through? As soon as Sue came out, he went in and held Ellie close as she cried. He could tell she was as devastated as he was as they observed the still, small form of the tiny baby boy who would never have the chance to run and play. It was a complete shock to both of them. Ellie had been fine during the time she was expecting. There was no indication that anything was wrong. Finally, Ellie told Jonny to send David and Sue home.

"Before they go, could you get them to ask if we could bury the little one over at the Dunn Cemetery? That's where I'd like to have him buried if it's possible."

Jonny followed his wife's instructions and had the baby buried in the little church cemetery. Ellie was so blue all winter after that. When springtime came, he hoped it would help her spirits, but she was still struggling in mid-August.

The town of Lynch was owned by U.S. Steel, and by 1939 it was a booming coal town. The company built many homes in the town, along with a hospital and a nice theater, for the convenience of the miners. Jonny had taken Ellie to the theater a few times, but nothing seemed to excite her.

Recently, they had discovered she was expecting a child again, and it seemed to produce both excitement and fear in her. She needed something to focus on other than the baby during the coming months.

"How would you like to move out of this place?" Jonny said one day a few weeks after they realized they would be adding a little one to their family.

"Where? When?" asked Ellie.

"We can move into one of those houses up on Hight Street that we were looking at the other day. I talked to my boss, and he said he had one that would be free next week, and we could have it if we wanted it. We can go look at it tomorrow. I think you'll like it."

"That's wonderful. Maybe we can get in and get settled before the baby comes." Ellie didn't sound too excited, but at least she was positive about it.

On Saturday they went to look at the house. They both agreed it was perfect for them. The price was not much more than they were currently paying, but it was a cute little white frame house that had had only one other occupant since it was built.

"Let's take it," said Ellie. Jonny agreed to tell his boss they wanted it.

They moved in the following week. The house was small but much better than where they had been living. Jonny was pleased that he'd made an effort to make a happy home for Ellie and the little one, but he knew Ellie still worried because the job he had was so dangerous.

Ellie had made an appointment to see a doctor a few weeks before it was time for the baby to come. Both she and Jonny had decided they wanted a doctor to assist at the birth because of their fear after what had happened at the birth of their first baby. The doctor agreed to come to their home, which was just minutes from the hospital.

When the baby girl was born, Jonny was just as happy as Ellie was. His own child! Joy! That's what they both wanted to call her, because she was, after all, a source of real joy to both of them. Jonny knew that most men did not want to have much to do with taking care of children, but he loved to hold Joy and kept asking Ellie if she needed help with her. Unfortunately, this new addition didn't sleep much, and she cried a lot.

After three weeks, they took her to the doctor, and he said, "She's not getting enough nourishment. We need to change her to a bottle instead of breast milk." They tried that for a few weeks, but after six weeks Joy was still not gaining weight. Then they decided that maybe the cow's milk was not agreeing with her. "I think we need to see if she can tolerate goat's milk," the doctor said. That seemed to do the trick, and Joy seemed to be well and happy after that.

Jonny and Ellie and their baby continued to live in Lynch, and he continued to work in the coal mines for nearly a year before he earned his certificate for completing the eighth grade. Mr. Orr brought it to him one day at the store. During that time Jonny had not thought much about his hope to someday learn how to be a welder.

Meanwhile, however, he had begun to settle into his life as a husband and father. He truly enjoyed seeing his little girl's eyes light up when he walked into the room in the evenings or picked her up out of her bed in the mornings. When Joy was about four months old, Ellie told Jonny she was not feeling well one Saturday morning and asked him if he could feed Joy and get her dressed for the day.

Jonny was more than happy to at least act like he could do it easily, but he was a little worried. He'd not seen Ellie sick for a long time. When had she been sick before? Oh! Could it be that she was expecting another baby? Surely not—they had barely gotten used to Joy. It seemed like only a few months ago that she had finally got on a diet that agreed with her. It wasn't long, though, before they were sure they would be having another mouth to feed in a few months.

After a traumatic death inside the mines one week, Jonny and Ellie were scheduled to make a trip down to Laurel County. On the way there Ellie expressed her concern about Jonny's safety in the mines. When they arrived at Thomas' house, he was sitting on the porch waiting, as usual. After a few minutes of small talk, Thomas asked Jonny to follow him down to the barn where he needed to feed the mules.

"Jonny," he asked, "would you and Ellie have any interest in returning to Laurel County to live?"

"I think we'd love to live back in Laurel County, Thomas, but what would I do? I have to make a living, you know, and I haven't had anyone asking me to work down here."

"I know there isn't anything right now, but if you lived here, you might find something."

"Are you wanting us to live here with you?" asked Jonny.

"No. I mean, you'd certainly be welcome to live with me, but I was thinking that I have this piece of land up the road there. It only has a small shack on it now, but if you wanted the land, I could deed it over to you, and you could build on the land."

"That sounds like a really good idea, but I just don't know what I'd do here," said Jonny.

"Well, think about it. And also think about moving here and continuing to work at the mine until you could find something here…just a thought," said Thomas. "I won't mention it to Ellie, but you can tell her what I said, and you all can decide."

Jonny couldn't determine whether Thomas was acting out of a longing for his daughter to be nearby or if he was just offering them a good deal on a piece of land, but one way or another it was a move he was tempted to make. He had hoped to get back to Laurel County all along, and the thought of building a home and raising a family there fit in with his own desire for life.

By the time they returned to Lynch that Sunday, Jonny was ready to get Ellie's reaction to the idea. The moment he told her, he could tell she wanted to do it, but she asked him what he thought.

"Well, it fits in perfectly with what I'd like to do in some ways, but I just hate leaving you down there with the babies so much of the time with no help, especially if I have to continue to work in Lynch."

"What if we could find someone to stay with me during the week?"

"Well, who would you get?"

"I was thinking about one of my nieces. They might like to stay. Maybe one or two of them could trade out, one staying one week and the other staying the next week."

"Aren't they in school?" Jonny asked.

"Yes, but they could come over after school and spend the night. That's the main thing—I'd just hate to be there alone at night."

Jonny thought for a moment. "I don't know. We can think about it and decide for sure before we go back down there."

The news of another baby had both confirmed the fact that they wanted to be back in Laurel County and aroused some concern about making sure Jonny had a stable job. He remembered the trouble his own family had had with so many children and his dad not having a job. When he expressed those concerns to Ellie, she tried to reassure him.

"Jonny, just remember that you are not your dad. Remember how you've always said that you've never gone without a job? And you haven't. You're such a hard worker, and you are healthy. I think you'll continue to be like that. And of course now that you have a little more education, that will help you continue to keep a job."

After a while they both agreed that moving back "home" would be a good idea for them. Of course, they'd eventually need money to build a house there, but at first they could live in the little shack that was already there.

When they arrived at Thomas' that weekend, the first thing Ellie said was, "Dad, we've decided to move back down here near you."

"I'm glad to hear it," he said. "When do you plan to move?"

"We want to wait until after the baby is born. We're hoping to move in late summer or early fall, before it gets too cold."

"That'll be good. I'll try to get that little shack fixed up a bit before you come."

"Can we go look at it tomorrow?" Ellie asked. She was feeling better the last week or so, and it was the first time Jonny had seen her that excited about anything in a long time, maybe since she'd lost the first baby. Even though she obviously loved Joy, she had often continued to be rather somber. But now she seemed genuinely excited, and it made him happy to see it.

The next morning after breakfast they headed over to the little shack to take a look. It was small and shabby, but Jonny and Ellie looked around the two little rooms and pointed out things they could do to make them work and also talked about how their furniture would fit. Thomas was also telling them what he could do to make the little house livable. He was obviously excited about having his daughter closer home.

By the time Jonny and Ellie left Laurel County that weekend, they had a plan to move a few months after the new baby was born. That spring there was genuine excitement in their home. They were ready for the new little one, or at least as ready as one can be for a new baby when the older one is just a year old.

Grace was born at home on May 1, with a doctor in attendance. She was a perfectly healthy baby. The next-door neighbor, whom Joy loved, had kept her that night. When Joy looked at her little sister the next day, she cried. What was this intruder doing in her mother's arms? After about a week, Ellie realized there was more wrong with Joy than jealousy. She started running a fever, and she was obviously sick. On Friday evening when Jonny came home from work, Ellie spoke to him about Joy.

"You need to take Joy to the doctor. Something is wrong with her, and I can't leave the baby to take her," Ellie said. "Look how fast she's breathing. And don't you think her neck looks swollen?"

"Yeah, she sounds bad when she coughs too. And yes, her neck does look puffed up a little. I'll just take her over to the hospital. What do I tell the doctor, though? I haven't been with her as much as you have."

"Well, she's been crying a lot, and she's had a fever for three days straight," said Ellie. "That's about all. Oh, she hasn't eaten anything much at all today. I tried to give her a bottle, but she wouldn't take it—just turned her face away."

Jonny bundled her up and walked to the hospital a short distance from where they lived. She cried almost all the way, despite Jonny's attempts to calm her. Fortunately, the doctor was able to see them right away. He examined Joy and immediately began to try to determine her problem.

"I hate to tell you this," he said, "but I'm pretty sure she has a disease called diphtheria."

"What does that mean? What can you do?" Jonny asked. He was scared because he had no idea about the illness, but he had heard that some children had died from it.

"Well, I don't want you to be alarmed, but it is a very serious illness. However, we do have medicine for it that can be given here in the hospital. She'll need to stay here a few days, though."

Jonny panicked at the thought of his little girl having to be admitted to the hospital. "I don't know what we'll do. My wife had a baby last week, and she can't leave her to come here. I don't know whether I can get off from work either. But if she has to be here, we'll just have to find a way. Does she need to stay here right now? I don't have any way to contact my wife."

"Well, the quicker she gets treatment, the quicker we can get her well." The doctor looked around. "Do you have a phone?"

"No, we don't, so there's no way to phone her." Jonny felt scared.

"Do you have friends you could contact to go tell your wife? If so, you can use the phone over there to call them."

"There's a couple next door to us who would probably go tell her. They have a phone, and I guess I could call them. I think I wrote their number down somewhere. He looked in his wallet and found the phone number. When the wife answered, Jonny explained the situation to her, and she agreed to go talk to Ellie.

"If Ellie can come over here, is there a number we can call you back?" she asked Jonny.

Jonny looked down at the phone and saw the number. He read it to her and then went back to Joy, who was crying and reaching for him. He picked her up and held her until the doctor could arrange for her to be admitted to the hospital.

Meanwhile, Ellie called him back, and they worked it out so that Jonny could stay there with Joy through the weekend. On Monday morning he got his neighbor to come to the hospital while he went to explain his situation to his boss. Fortunately, the man was willing to give him some time off to stay at the hospital.

Joy was hospitalized for a week before the doctors got the diphtheria under control. Jonny and Ellie's neighbor came to the hospital and stayed with Joy for a while every day while Jonny went home and reported to Ellie and got a little sleep. Most of the time he had to stay awake at night because Joy was fussy and afraid. She didn't like for anyone to touch her except her dad.

"You must be a good daddy," said one of the nurses after Joy had fought to stay with him when the nurse had tried to feed her.

"Well, at least she knows me," said Jonny with a smile.

It was a rough week, but finally Joy was released from the hospital and back home with Ellie and Grace.

CHAPTER 22

Fortunately for the family, Grace was a healthy, happy baby, having no issues, but Jonny and Ellie could see that two babies 13 months apart was going to be a challenge. When Grace was about two months old, they made the move back to Laurel County.

"There's no way you can do this by yourself when I'm working in Lynch the whole week," Jonny told Ellie the week they were packing to move.

"I guess that's right," agreed Ellie. "But it may take the first week just to line up someone to help me."

When they were moving in, Ellie talked to her brother Pete about asking one of his daughters to stay with her that first week.

"I'm sure any one of them would love to," he said. "But they're all down with a cold right now. Maybe by next week they'll feel better. You don't want your babies to get sick. That's just asking for more trouble."

"Let me see if one of my brothers could come and stay this next week," offered Jonny. "They probably won't be a lot of help, but at least you wouldn't be here by yourself," he said, laughing.

One of Jonny's brothers did come and stay with Ellie and the babies during the first week. After that, Pete's daughters Rita and Jane developed a routine of coming after school each day to stay through the night. They helped Ellie with the evening chores, cooking supper, and getting the little ones ready for bed. At first Jane came on Monday and Tuesday, and Rita came on Wednesday and Thursday. On Friday they would rotate, doing the same thing, except not spending the night, because Jonny would usually get home around the girls' bedtime. Sometimes Lucy, Pete's youngest daughter, would come on Friday to give one of the other girls a break.

Ellie soon learned that Jane was the one who enjoyed staying with her the most, so she was not too surprised when Rita left one Thursday, saying she would not be able to come the next week.

"What's wrong?" asked Ellie.

"Well, I just won't be able to come. Maybe you can get someone else to do it."

Ellie was pretty sure there was no reason except that Rita just didn't like coming, so she said nothing else about it. Friday afternoon was Jane's turn to come, and Ellie thought she might mention it, but she didn't.

When Jonny came home Friday night, Ellie told him what Rita had said. "I can probably do it by myself. After all, it's just two nights."

"No, I don't want you to do that," he said. "You never know what might happen, and you'd need somebody here."

"Well, there's a girl at church who might help me those two nights, so I'll ask her Sunday."

Jonny made Ellie promise to have someone lined up by Tuesday, and Ellie said she would. She was a little worried when the girl she asked at church said she could not help.

Jane came in on Monday afternoon saying that if it was okay, she'd like to be Ellie's helper all the time! Ellie was so happy that she gave Jane a big hug. "Of course it's okay, Honey. In fact, it's perfect!"

Jonny was listening to the radio one Saturday evening when he heard the announcer say they were really needing welders in Baltimore, Maryland. He also said they were training welders every week at the Bethlehem-Fairfield Shipyards to work on Liberty Ships. It just so happened that the mine where Jonny worked had closed that Monday and Tuesday because of a cave-in near the front of the mine. He immediately considered that an opportunity to find out if he might be able to train and work as a welder. Ellie wasn't crazy about the idea, but she agreed it might be worth trying. He left early Sunday morning, taking with him what he'd need for the week if he should stay. He promised to write a letter to her the first day he was there if he decided to stay.

The long drive to Baltimore was different than his long drives from Michigan to Tulsa and from Tulsa back to Kentucky. On those trips he had dealt with fear and uncertainty and disappointment. On this drive he had a purpose. He also knew that when he went back, he had a wife and two children who would welcome him home with open arms. Jonny wanted to see if there were possibilities for a better life for all of them. But even if it turned out not to be a good thing, he knew he could go back home. The trip seemed much shorter because he was happy. When he arrived at his destination, it was late in the evening, and his plan was to find a hotel for the night. Baltimore was a little like Tulsa, so he was not unfamiliar with his possibilities.

On the outskirts of the city, he saw a familiar hotel sign and stopped. When he entered and went up to the desk, there were rooms available. Ready for some rest, he booked the room. He was hardly aware of what the room was like. All he noticed was the bed. The next morning when he awoke, he saw that the sun was already shining. After a quick breakfast at a nearby café, he headed over to the shipyards to see if there was indeed a need for workers. The manager at the hotel had written the instructions about how to get to the shipyards. Jonny was to go to the south shore of the middle branch of the Patapsco River, which serves as the Baltimore Harbor. The hotel manager had also written that the shipyards were owned by the Bethlehem Shipbuilding Company, created by the Bethlehem Steel Corporation. When Jonny got close to the area, he began to see some of the landmarks the guy at the hotel had mentioned. Soon he saw what looked like the building the man had described.

Baltimore Harbor was old. The area had been expanded in 1916 to house massive shops before World War I, but it was empty during the depression in the 1930s. Now they were using it for one of two emergency shipyards, according to the hotel manager. Jonny was trying to remember all the man had said when he walked into the office to ask for a job.

When a burly, middle-aged man appeared through his office door, he looked at Jonny, smiled, and said, "Hello, young man. My name is Johnson. What can I do for you?"

"I need a job."

"What kind of work can you do?"

"I'll do anything you need, but I'm not a skilled worker—yet."

"Are you strong and coordinated? Are your eyes good?"

Jonny wondered what the man was getting at. He wasn't sure how to respond, but he said, "Well, yes, I'm strong and coordinated. I've worked in the coal mines and in the oil fields. And my eyesight has never been a problem."

"The reason I'm asking is that one of the things we're needing is welders. They are training welders all the time now. It's an outside school, and I wonder if you'd be interested in becoming a welder."

"That's exactly what I'd hoped to be able to do. Do I need to have a certain level of education to train to be a welder?"

"We like for you to have at least an eighth-grade education."

"I have that," said Jonny, feeling proud of his accomplishments during the year.

"Okay, let's go into the office here and get you signed up then," Mr. Johnson said, turning around and heading inside. Then he stopped and added, "The only problem is they just started a training session a few days ago, so you may have to wait a few weeks. Are you employed anywhere now?"

"No. I just got in town yesterday."

Jonny must have looked upset, because the man said, "It's okay. I'll help you find something for a few weeks."

They walked into the office, where they learned that the six-week session had indeed only started recently, so it would be a while before Jonny could start training. Mr. Johnson promised to help him find a job if he'd come back to the shipyards the next morning. He told Jonny he'd check around to see if he could find anyone needing temporary help somewhere—maybe a restaurant or something.

Jonny went back to the hotel and got instructions about finding a more permanent place to stay in Baltimore. By nightfall he had found a boarding house where he could rent a room at a low price. He took his clothes and other supplies in and got comfortable before taking out his pencil and paper to write a letter to Ellie. He knew she'd be expecting one in the next day or two, letting her know he'd arrived in Baltimore safely. He wished the news was a little better about the job, though. He sat there for a bit, trying to think of a positive way to describe the situation. Finally, he picked up his pencil and began to write.

> *Dear Ellie,*
>
> *I made it safely to Baltimore last night with no problems. I miss you and my babies. Give them hugs and kisses from Daddy. I went to the shipyards today and talked to a man who told me that they would train me to be a welder. The only problem is that I can't start training for several weeks, so during that time I won't have work unless I can find something here. The man said he'd help me find something while I wait, but that means I can't come home, and then I'll have to take the training and I can't come during that time either. Since it will be about six weeks before I can start training and it is a six-week training, that will be nearly three months. I am sorry. Maybe this was a mistake. I love you and my babies so much. Well, tomorrow I'll see what I can do. Please write to me and tell me what you think about all this.*
>
> *Love,*
> *Jonny*

The next day he went to the shipyard to look for Mr. Johnson. The man handed Jonny a slip of paper with the name and address of a restaurant on it. "Go down to this restaurant and tell them Johnson sent you," he said. "You'll have to go down to Pratt Street. I think they'll let you work there for a few weeks."

"Thank you so much. I'll do that right now." Even though he was disappointed in not getting to start at the shipyards immediately, Jonny felt hopeful that he might at least have a job. The only problem was that he'd not be able to go home for so long. But he was determined to make enough money to keep Ellie and his girls well fed. He remembered how his own family had struggled just to have food to eat. He was a little afraid of how Ellie would take the news when she got his letter, though.

It was getting close to lunchtime when Jonny arrived at Connolly's Seafood House, at Pratt Street and Pier 5. The place was bustling with waiters trying to serve their customers. By this time he was hungry, so he decided to eat lunch there before he talked to the manager.

Seated near the entrance to the kitchen, Jonny hoped he might find an employee to ask how to apply for a job. When his stomach was full, he got up and approached an employee as she was heading back into the kitchen.

"Excuse me, Miss, but could you tell me where I could apply for a job here?"

She looked at him for a moment. "Yes, I could. And we could sure use some help right now."

She led him over to the side where another door had a small sign that read "Office" on it. She knocked on the door, and they heard "Come on in" from inside the room.

The waitress opened the door and said to the person inside, "Someone here wants to see you about a job," and then she left Jonny to fend for himself.

When he entered the room, a gray-haired, middle-aged lady sat at a desk piled up with books, papers, and lots of unopened mail. She sighed and looked up at him with a tired smile and asked, "What can I do for you?"

"I talked to Mr. Johnson at the shipyards this morning. I just arrived in Baltimore two days ago, and I need some work. Johnson said to come here and tell you he sent me. Would you have anything I could do here at least for a few weeks until I can begin training as a welder?"

"I might," the lady said. "Would you be interested in washing dishes?"

"Sure. I washed dishes in a hospital in Tulsa, Oklahoma, for a while. I was pretty good at it. Also, I have had to help my wife back in Kentucky quite a bit. We have two little girls, so there's a lot to do around the house," he said, smiling at her.

So, Jonny took the job washing dishes at the cafeteria. After working out a schedule with the lady, he felt better about his decision to stay in Baltimore. The first week was a busy one, but finally he got time to write Ellie a short letter and tell her he had a job. He waited anxiously for her reply and was pleased when he saw her letter in his mailbox.

Dearest Jonny,

I got your letter yesterday. Sure pleased to hear from the only one I care for. I looked for a letter today but didn't get any. Seems like I want to get one every day (Ha). Hope you don't stay away too long. I'm crazy to see you now.

I'm just like you darling, I'm getting awful tired of this staying away from you, but I'm trying to pass it off the best I can cause I know we can't do any better at present.

Poor little Joy came and laid her little hands on my paper and wanted me to mark around them. I took her to the doctor this morning. Something bit her on the jaw yesterday and her whole neck and face is swelled and just as red. I thought it was a mosquito, for the mosquitos and gnats have just about eat both of the kids up. But Doctor Whitis didn't seem to think it was. He seems to think it must have been a rat or spider. He gave her some medicine. It don't look much better this morning, but she seems very pert.

The kids are both asleep and Jane is writing to someone. She came back yesterday but I stayed by myself Sunday night, and I got along pretty good. Dad milked for me. My cow gives almost two gallons of milk every night and not so much in the morning. My pigs are growing pretty good. I got enough cucumbers over there this morning to can six quarts. I'm going to try to get me some peaches. I think someone is going to bring a load down in this part tomorrow.

Well, honey, I'll try to take care of that note. I've got my business kindly mixed up. I sent part of that money to the bank by Dad and he put it in the wrong account, and I sent the rest by David and he got it straightened out. I told Dad how to put it in, but I reckon he forgot. It's all okay now. I sent word to David to come and see if he could get this old car started. I thought if he could, I'd get him to take us to the store this evening.

I haven't spent anything except paid Jane and paid $1.50 to the doctor for Joy. I haven't bought any ice since you left. I miss you so bad about seeing to all these little things. We're due some more canning sugar but I don't know how to go about getting it. Didn't you have a coupon of some kind that you were supposed to take back to get the rest of it?

Don't worry about us. We are doing okay. Naturally, I hate that you have to be gone that long, but it's better than not having a job.

With love from your wife and babies,
Ellie

Jonny thought about all she said and then began to write to tell her a little more about his job washing dishes. He was glad Ellie understood why he'd have to be gone longer than he'd planned. At the same time he wished she was not having to work so hard. He was lucky to have a wife who loved him, and he was especially thankful for his two little girls. Maybe things would work out all right.

Dear Ellie,

I got your letter today. Sounds like you are very busy with the girls and with gardening and all. Don't worry about the bank stuff and the car. Well, I got a job washing dishes in a restaurant called Connolly's Seafood. As you know, I have never been much for fish, but when they fry it up like they do, it tastes okay. The man at the shipyards told me about the place. I went down and had lunch and then talked to the lady who owns the place. The only thing about it is that I'll have to work on weekends, but I knew that was a possibility. Anyway, I won't be able to come home until after my welders' training. I'm sorry, Honey. I just hate not being able to come home for that long. Try to write often and keep telling Joy that she's Daddy's Doll. I hope she'll remember me when I come home, but I'm afraid she won't. I'll write as often as I can.

Love,
Jonny

One night after working a long shift, Jonny was exhausted. Before he went into his apartment, he checked his mail, and sure enough there was a letter from Ellie. He sat down to read it as soon as he entered the living room.

Hello Sweetie,

Just a few more lines this morning to let you know we are still O.K. The baby slept better last night than she has ever slept in her life. I never had to get up with her except give her a bottle twice, and she's so sweet this morning, laughing at everything that moves. Wish you could see her.

Joy is getting fat as a pig again. She eats all the time and little Grace has been awful good today. I think she is getting better but the poor little thing sure hasn't been doing any good.

Honey, don't worry about us. We are all right. Sue is washing for me so I don't have much to do except tend to the kids, and when the baby is well they aren't much trouble.

Pete was talking about having some hay baled. I think he said they loaded about 69 bales for his part at one place, but I don't know if that was all he cut or not.

I got your letter yesterday. I was surprised to find that you were working in a restaurant, especially a seafood restaurant. I'm afraid you'll get too fat working there, for I know you'll manage to get plenty to eat. Sure hope so. Don't know how I'd like a big fat man (Ha). I guess it would be O.K. if it was you though. Hope you've had a good day.

The ones who love you most,
Your wife and babies

Jonny laughed when he read Ellie's letter. He was glad she seemed to be in a good mood. Even though he worked long hours, especially on the weekends, he enjoyed working with the others at Connolly's, and staying busy made the days and weeks pass by quickly. Soon it was the week before he would be starting his training to become a welder. When he mentioned it to his supervisor at Connolly's, she seemed to have forgotten he had come as a temporary employee.

"You mean you're just quitting?"

"Well, you know, I will be starting my welder's training at the shipyards next week. I might be able to help out a little from time to time, but I really don't know much about my schedule."

"Could you still help out some on the weekends?"

I think so, but I'm not sure. Tell you what… I'll talk to Mr. Johnson tomorrow, and then I'll know what I can do."

After talking to Mr. Johnson, he was able to report to his restaurant supervisor that he could help some on the weekends. He had known they didn't want him to leave town during the training, but he wasn't sure why. Mr. Johnson said Jonny would probably be free most weekends, but they didn't want him to go out of town because they might want the trainees to stay late on Friday to finish their work, and they might even have to work occasional weekends.

He wrote Ellie a letter telling her he would be starting the training soon and it would not be too long before he could come home.

The first day of welding school was a big day for Jonny. His excitement was squelched a little by the old feeling of inferiority that used to plague him all the time, though, but he decided to put that aside and think in a positive way.

The welding instructor looked friendly enough as he came into the room full of mostly young men, with a few women scattered around the room. He was carrying several items that Jonny assumed were necessary for his explaining how to be a welder. Jonny approached him and asked if he needed help bringing anything in.

"Sure, just follow me out here, and I'll load you up with more gear."

Jonny followed him outside and helped bring another load into the building, which was situated just outside the shipyard. It was a temporary-looking structure designed to allow individual students the opportunity to practice their welding skills safely.

The instructor arranged all the items on the stage. Then he looked up at the group, ready to start class. "I'll begin with what you'll need to wear when welding. It's one of the most important parts of your training," he said, which brought a ripple of laughter in the audience.

He waited a few seconds and then said, "I know, I know. You hadn't expected me to begin with clothing, had you? But if you don't get this part right, you might not be around for the other important things. Welding can be a dangerous job if you don't know the rules. One of the rules is that when you weld, you must always wear a welding shield. It looks like this," he said, as he held up a big shield with lenses to protect the eyes. "This protects the head, face, and eyes from the sparks that often come off the welding rods. You see the lenses that go over the eyes here. This shield is always needed, whether you're doing welding on a flat surface, round surface, or something overhead."

"What about our hair?" asked one of the women.

"That's a good question," said the instructor. "If your hair is long, you'll need to wear it up in a bun or something. I've seen women's hair catch on fire. The sparks can be dangerous. Just like you need to wear a shield every day, women need to make sure their hair is up and out of the way. Some days that may be more important than others, but during training you won't know for sure what we'll be doing each day, so you'll need to protect your hair all the time."

He moved over and picked up a pair of gloves.

"The second part of clothing you'll need in any kind of welding are the gloves. Some people have been badly burned because they forgot their gloves and thought they could get by without them for one shift. Because of this, you will be issued these in class today, and you will never be allowed into class without these two items—the shield and the gloves."

A few hands went up, and the instructor answered questions posed by some of the young men and women. Then he walked around to the other side of the stage.

"The following items may or may not be needed, depending on what type of welding you're doing for a specific job, but for our purposes in class, you will be issued these as they are needed."

Then he held up a suede jacket. "This jacket is important if you're welding overhead. It protects your shoulders and back from sparks falling down on you."

The instructor showed a few other items of clothing and then turned to the other items lying on the table on the other side of the platform. "We'll be covering a number of ways to weld. Some of you may not actually do all these kinds of welding once you have a job. We'll start with the rod welders' tools." He held up a rod. "Most of you will at some time have to use this tool. It is used for welding large flat surfaces, and most often to attach large slabs of steel that will eventually become the sides of the ships." After he showed the students the various kinds of welding tools and explained how each worked, he began to describe what the following days would be like.

Jonny was excited. The instructor talked about different ways their knowledge and experience in the welding area could be beneficial, no matter where they lived or what they happened to be doing. When he got to the part about pipeline welding, Jonny knew it was possible that some day he might be able to use that skill in the area where he lived. It made him optimistic.

After he finished his training at the end of October, Jonny was able to make a short trip home before he started work. When he got home, the girls were a little unwilling to welcome him back, but of course he understood. After a short time, Joy seemed to warm up to him, but it took Grace a little longer. It was like that throughout the winter. He would work a few weeks and come home for the weekend. The girls would get used to him, and then he'd leave again. Although he liked his work and Jane was helping Ellie, he felt like it would be so much better if they could all be together.

The week after he returned from Kentucky, he was assigned to do some rod welding for a few days. When he was having to weld overhead, he remembered the instructor had emphasized wearing the suede jacket. Unfortunately, in his hurry to be sure he put the jacket on, he had taken off his gloves and forgotten to put them back on. As he worked, he suddenly realized his hands were getting burned. He tried to stop, but not quickly enough. He felt like a fool. One of his co-workers saw what happened, and before Jonny knew it, he was on his way to the clinic. They bandaged his hands and reprimanded him for failing to wear his gloves. For several days he dealt with the pain, and he never forgot to wear his gloves again.

While they were apart, Jonny and Ellie wrote letters often. Jonny always enjoyed Ellie's letters telling him about his little girls. Ellie tried to remain positive about his absence, but it was obvious she was having a hard time taking care of everything.

Dear Ellie,

How are you and my babies doing? I'm liking my work fine, but I made a mistake and forgot to put my gloves back on the other day and burned my hands. They're still pretty sore, but I think they're okay. The supervisors weren't too sympathetic with me because they'd emphasized during class that we should always wear our gloves. Anyway, I'm going to be fine. I hope you and the girls are okay too.

Love from your only fellow,
Jonny

Jonny knew that Ellie was one person who would sympathize with him and not want him to get hurt. Of course, he also knew there was nothing she could do about the fact he'd burned himself with the welding equipment, but at least she'd care.

Hello Sweetheart,

I will drop you a few lines tonight as I'm thinking of you as usual. I wonder how my sweet little man is tonight—Okay, I sure hope. This leaves us all well. The baby has been sleeping so good the last few nights, but she has been crying on me again tonight. I reckon she just has a little cold. It's after 10 o'clock and I just have got her off to sleep. I went to town today and paid that note off. I went up with Dad.

I sure hate about you burning your hands. You must be careful darling and not do that anymore. I don't want anything to happen to my little man. Honey, I'll be so tickled for you to come home. Don't guess I'll ever get through loving you. I can't see how I was lucky enough to get the sweetest man in the world anyway, do you? That's one thing I can say. I'm satisfied with my choice. I never think of caring for anyone but you.

I haven't time to write much. I have to send this by Jane as she goes to school tomorrow. I don't know what I'm going to do. I can't hardly make out with a kid going to school. She has to leave so early, and I can't get out no where. Can hardly even go to the mail box.

I did go to the mail box after I came back from town, and I got your letter. Sure pleased to hear from my darling and know you are still okay. Say, Sweetheart, I'm getting so sleepy I can't hardly hold my eyes open, so I believe I'll stop and go to bed. Maybe it won't be long till you are home and I'll just tell you how much I love you. I like it better that way anyhow, don't you?

So bye and be good till I see you again.

With Love,
Your wife and babies

Jonny wrote to Ellie and asked her if she had enough money to buy extra clothes for the babies. He thought she probably did, but he knew she tried to save all she could, and it was important to him that they had what they needed. Before he could get the letter mailed, he received another letter from Ellie.

Dearest Jonny,

Just a few words tonight to let you know we are all okay, and certainly hope it finds my man the same. Boy it sure has been cold here today. Dad and David came down here yesterday and put Dad's battery in the car, but it still wouldn't start. They took it up on the road and pushed it with David's truck, but it wouldn't take off. They said a guy looked at it and said there was just some little something wrong with it, a short or something, and said if I'd get a battery for it, he'd come over and find out what was wrong with it and fix it. I sent and got a battery by Pete today.

Grace has got better, but still coughs pretty bad. I got your letter yesterday. Sure pleased to hear from you and know you are well. Dad sold his calves yesterday and got two hundred and seven dollars for the four.

I got a notice from the bank yesterday, so I'm sending it on to you. I see it's due the 20th of the month.

David said Sue was sick with tonsillitis.

I wish you didn't have to work on Sunday. It worries me.

Honey, you must get you some clothes to keep you warm. I don't want you to get sick away off out there. Seems like I've been uneasy about you for the last few days. I hope you are not sick.

If you come home at Christmas, it won't be long now, so maybe I can stand it that much longer without seeing you. (ha) I don't guess you will know Grace. She doesn't look at all like she did when you left, but she's sweet like her Daddy and smart like her mother (Ha, Ha).

Joy is standing here by me and I said, "Whose sweet honey?" and she said, "Daddy's doll." Every time I start petting the baby, she begins hollering "Daddy's Doll" I think she thinks it spites me for her to say that, and she's got so jealous of the baby. She don't want me to touch her. She got one of your pictures the other night and you ought to have seen her kissing it.

Well, Sweetheart, I'll close as I don't know anything else to write. So good-bye, be good, and be careful, and take good care of your sweet self and come home soon.

As ever, the ones that love you best,
Ellie and Babies

Jonny read the letter and sat there looking at it. Ellie's letters were always interesting to him because they told him about the girls and how they were doing. He was glad Joy remembered she was "Daddy's doll." He worried about his wife and little babies and was thankful she had both her family and David and Sue helping her some. He was about to fall asleep, so he got out his pencil and wrote her back before he got ready for bed.

Dearest Ellie,

Thank you for writing me about what you and the babies are doing. I'm glad Grace is sleeping well and Jane is with you at night. I still worry that you don't have enough help. We'll talk about what we could do when I'm home for Christmas. Just a week away.

I'll get me some warmer clothes tomorrow after work, so don't worry about me. Tell the babies Daddy loves them, and tell Joy that she's still Daddy's doll. I'm sorry this is so short, but I'm really sleepy tonight, and I have to get up early tomorrow morning. I will stop here and get ready for bed.

Yours forever,
Jonny

Jonny tore out the piece of notebook paper he'd written on and folded the letter, and then took one of the envelopes and a stamp out of the bedside table drawer and addressed the letter to Ellie. He licked the stamp and put it on the envelope, then sealed the envelope and placed it on the table beside his bed so he wouldn't forget it the next morning. He could mail it at his workplace.

He couldn't believe that in just a few days he'd be headed home for Christmas. He'd have almost a week with Ellie and the girls! Last year Joy was only about nine months old, but this year she'd be old enough to get a little excited about the Christmas tree and toys.

"What are you doing during Christmas?" one of the other workers asked him at Connolly's on Saturday when he was washing dishes.

"I'm going home to see my wife and babies," Jonny answered, with a big smile.

"Where do they live?" asked the young lady.

"In Kentucky," he replied.

"Oh, then you must be really excited. How old are your kids?"

"One is almost two years old, and the other is just about eight months old. I think this will be an exciting time for Joy, who will be two soon."

"I have a two-year-old. She is definitely excited this Christmas," said a young lady who had been listening to their conversation. "We put up our tree yesterday, and she is fascinated by it. I'm afraid she'll pull on the decorations and get hurt or pull the tree down! I have to watch her all the time."

Jonny wondered if Ellie had put up a tree. If she hadn't, he'd do so when he got home.

On Monday evening when he got off work, he went straight to his apartment and packed so that he could leave for Laurel County right after work on Tuesday. He was excited because he had bought some affordable children's books for the girls and packed them away in his suitcase. He knew Ellie would like them.

At about three o'clock on Tuesday, Johnny was finishing a welding job when he heard a sound behind him. Mr. Johnson appeared at his side and said, "Hey, man. You don't have time to start another job. Why don't you just head on down toward Kentucky when you finish this?"

Jonny gave him a big smile. "That would be wonderful if I could do that. It would mean I could get out of town before traffic gets bad. Thank you!"

"You have a good Christmas with your family now."

Jonny finished his work and got in his car. The trip was long but not nearly as long as it would have seemed if he'd had to stay at work for two more hours. Tired but happy, several hours later he pulled up in front of the little shack. He was surprised to see the faint glow of a light in the kitchen. Pulling his suitcase out of the back of the car, he approached the front door. Just as he raised his hand to knock, the door opened, and Ellie stood in the doorway to welcome him.

"Oh, I'm so glad to see you! I actually thought it might be a few more hours," she said, not knowing he'd been able to leave work early that afternoon.

Jonny quickly put his suitcase down and embraced her. They stood there quietly for a moment, just enjoying the feeling of being together again and knowing he'd be home until after Christmas.

"They let me leave work a couple hours early… I'm starved. Is there something to eat by any chance?"

"As a matter of fact, there is," Ellie said, smiling. "I saved some of our supper."

As they walked into the kitchen, trying to be quiet and not wake the babies, Jonny saw several bowls of food on the table, including a plate with some cake. They chatted quietly while he ate until he was full.

When he got up from the table he told Ellie, "I want to show you something I got the girls for Christmas." He opened his suitcase and pulled out the bag and handed it to her. Ellie opened the bag carefully, and her eyes lit up when she saw the little picture books. She looked at each title: *The Poky Little Puppy, Baby's Book, Three Little Kittens.*

"Oh," she said, her eyes shining, "This is going to be the best Christmas ever!"

"I hoped you'd agree that these would be a perfect gift for our little girls," he said. "Put them away now, and you can decide tomorrow when to give them to our sweet babies."

"We'd better get to bed," Ellie encouraged. I know you're tired, and Grace has been waking up early the last few days, so it may not be long before morning comes around here."

As soon as Grace opened her eyes the next morning, Jonny was right there to pick her up, but she was not so sure about him. A frown came over her face, and she reached for Ellie. As Ellie took her, Joy sat up in bed and reached for Jonny. "Daddy's Doll" was all she said as she laid her head on his shoulder. Grace would come around in a day or so, he thought. At least Joy remembered him well.

Looking around the house later that morning, Jonny said, "Well, girls, we need a Christmas tree, don't we?"

"We do," agreed Ellie. "But I didn't think I could get one with these two babies. I saw one down by the fence out there," she said, pointing behind the house. "Why don't you go look at it and see if you think it'd work? There's an ax out there by the shed. Take it with you, and if you think we can use that tree, bring it in. Sue gave me some candles and tinsel she didn't need that we can use to decorate it."

When Jonny brought in the little cedar tree, Joy started jumping up and down. She didn't know what they were going to do with it, but she sensed it was an exciting time. Indeed, it was. It was the first time Jonny and Ellie had actually had a Christmas celebration in their home. The years before they had been either at Jonny's parents' house or at Ellie's dad's during Christmas. They would probably spend Christmas Day with their folks, but at least they'd be home during the next few days and could have their Christmas tree up and celebrate with their own little family.

Jonny put the Christmas tree up, and he and Ellie used the decorations Sue had given them along with a few ornaments Ellie had brought from her dad's. The girls were napping by the time their parents had begun decorating. When they finished, Ellie asked, "Do you think it's safe to light the candles? I'm afraid Joy will try to touch them or pull them off and get burned."

Jonny suggested, "What if I light them right before they wake up from their naps, just so they can see them for a few minutes before we put them out?"

Ellie laughed. "Well, that's probably what we will have to do. Joy may have a fit when you put them out, though."

Joy was ecstatic when she saw the candles. Jonny lifted her up and took her close enough to see the candles clearly but not close enough to touch them. "Look, Daddy, they're burning," she kept saying. Ellie held little Grace too. She seemed entranced and solemn at first and then got a big smile on her face, pointing toward the tree. After the girls had enjoyed the tree for a bit, Jonny distracted Joy with some other activity, and Ellie began to blow out the candles. Just as Ellie had predicted, Joy wasn't too happy when she saw that the candles were no longer lit, but she accepted it soon.

Throughout the afternoon Joy would point to the tree and say, "Daddy, lights," urging him to light them again. But, of course, he didn't.

After the kids were tucked in bed that night, Ellie got out the little books Jonny had bought. He could tell she was pleased with them.

"I was so excited when I saw these books," he said. "I don't remember that we had any children's picture books when I was little. Did you?"

"Not that I remember. These are wonderful. My teacher once said it was important to read to children when they are young," said Ellie. "I hope we can always read to Joy and Grace and that they will do well in school."

"I had been looking for some books to get them for Christmas, but most of them were two or three dollars apiece. The other day I was walking through a department store and looked down, and these were only 25 cents each. So that's why I went ahead and bought them. I want our girls to have lots of books."

"Me too." She looked at them again. "I guess we should give Grace the *Baby's Book*," she said. "But what about the others?"

"Well, Joy is so fascinated by kittens, so maybe we should give her *Three Little Kittens*," said Jonny.

"Okay. We could give Grace *The Poky Little Puppy* and Joy *The Little Red Hen*. It really won't matter, because we'll probably read all of them to both girls at the same time. But Joy seems to be a little selfish about sharing lately, so I guess we need to make it clear which ones are hers."

They wrapped the books in some red paper Ellie had found at her dad's a few weeks earlier and placed them under the tree, along with gifts they'd bought for each other.

"The Baptist church is having a Christmas program for the children tonight," said Ellie on Thursday. "Let's take the girls. I think Joy would especially like it, and I want her to learn some Christmas carols." Jonny agreed, and by that evening they had the family ready to go.

When they walked into the church, they saw a huge Christmas tree at the front with lots of decorations on it. Joy was awed by the sight. When the congregation began to sing "Joy to the World," both Ellie and Jonny sang along with the others, and the girls watched in silence. It was a festive occasion. Soon some of the children got up to sing. Both Joy and Grace were enthralled by the children as they sang and then acted out "Silent Night."

After the music ended, the pastor stood and read the story of Jesus's birth from the book of Luke in the Bible. At the end of the service, some of the other adults went to the front of the room, and the pastor announced there were treats for everyone. When they peeked into their brown paper bags, Jonny and Ellie found apples, oranges, and some candy.

By the time they got home, both girls were getting sleepy, so Jonny rocked Joy a little while, and Ellie rocked Grace. Soon both girls were in their beds fast asleep.

"Tomorrow is Christmas Day," said Ellie. "I guess we'd better plan to give the girls their books when they wake up in the morning."

"Yes, we'll start a tradition that Santa comes on Christmas Eve and leaves the presents under the tree," said Jonny.

"Of course, by next year we probably won't be able to leave them under the tree the night before because I know Joy will notice them," said Ellie, laughing.

"Yes! She notices everything. She may have noticed it tonight, but I think we'll get by with it this year."

Their first real Christmas with the two girls was a happy one, but all too quickly it was Sunday, and Jonny had to head back to Baltimore around noon.

CHAPTER 23

After Jonny finished his welder's training and became certified, he settled in as an employee in the Bethlehem-Fairfield Shipyards. The money was better, and the hours were too. The only problem was that Jonny would rather be working in Kentucky than in Baltimore. He knew it was important to stay in the shipyards for a while, but he longed to look for a job back home. His trip to Kentucky for Christmas had made that clear to him. One day he was talking to his boss, and his boss asked him where he was from.

"I have a wife and two children in Laurel County, Kentucky," he said. When he saw the blank look on his boss' face, he added, "London is the county seat of Laurel County."

"I thought I recognized that county name," he said. "I went to school with a guy from there. In fact, he just sent me a letter last week. He is a road construction worker, and he needs a welder. Would you be interested in a welding job permanently with him?"

"I would definitely be interested," Jonny told him. "But would the company let me go just after they had trained me?"

"I don't know. Maybe you'd have to wait another six months or so, just to fulfill some sort of requirement, but they can't keep you forever. I will check on it for you."

After about a week, Jonny asked his boss if he'd learned anything. "Not yet, but I'm thinking you'll have to stay until May. I will check with them again tomorrow," he promised.

The next day Jonny's boss verified that as long as he worked until May, he would not have any problem taking another job.

"But will the job with your friend still be open then?" asked Jonny.

"Oh, yes. I told him that I had the perfect employee, but he'd have to wait a few months before you could come."

"Guess what?" Jonny said to Ellie the next time he was home. "I can quit this job and come to work for a road construction company as a welder in May!"

"What? How did this happen? Tell me all about it!" she said.

Jonny told her about his conversations with his boss and how they'd found out that even though he'd trained with Bethlehem-Fairfield, they would release him from working there after six months if he had another job, especially since he had a wife and family there. The news made Ellie as happy as it had Jonny.

In 1942, the news was about the war in Europe. Soon after the bombing of Pearl Harbor in December of 1941. they had updated the Selective Service Training Act to include 18-year-olds. When it had first been signed into law in 1940, Jonny was the only one in his family who was eligible to go to war, and he was now married with a child. Now his brothers Steve and Owen were eligible. When Steve was called up and sent to off to West Africa in 1942, Mark tried to get his mother to sign something so that he could enlist, but Julia would not budge.

Since he wouldn't turn 18 until the spring of 1943, Mark was restless. One day he saw a sign in town advertising for young men to work at Kodiak Island, Alaska, where the U. S. government was building a naval air station.

He pointed it out to his brother Owen and two of their friends. "How much does it pay?" one of them asked.

"96 cents an hour," said Mark.

"Let's apply," said Owen.

Soon their plans were made. Fortunately, Jonny was home the weekend before they left. He, Ellie, and the girls joined the rest of his family in saying goodbye to the four boys who had signed up to go to Alaska and work for a six-month period.

Time passed quickly that spring, with Jonny coming home often for the weekend, and with each visit, he and Ellie became more excited about the possibilities for what they could do when he was working back in Kentucky.

In June of 1943, Jonny left Baltimore for the last time and moved back to Laurel County to begin work for Mr. Greer, who had just won a bid to do some road work.

The little shack where Jonny's family lived was small, and he and Ellie often talked about building a house nearby, but they agreed that could wait a few years if necessary. After about two years, when Jonny got home from work one evening, Pete was there with some news. A fellow who owned 200 acres of land not far from where he lived was willing to sell it for a good price.

"Does the land have a house on it?" Jonny asked.

"It does. You know, it's right on High Moore Ridge, just about a mile up the road from my house. You've seen it."

"Oh, yes. I know which one it is—a little white house."

"Yes. It's not new, but it's a lot better than that shack."

"I know it's a good price, but I don't have the money," Jonny said. "That's why we haven't tried to build yet. It'll take a while to get to the place where I have enough money to do something like that."

"What if you and I bought it together, and I started making payments on it? Later, you could start paying your part and pay me back. That would benefit us both, and we could divide it up, half and half." Jonny agreed and told Ellie about his agreement with Pete to buy the land.

"Can we really afford to do this? It sounds exciting," she said. "But I wouldn't want to move until we're actually paying Pete for our part."

Pete and Jonny signed an agreement about how they would divide up the land and Jonny would begin his payment by a certain date within the next year.

Jonny's work was not easy, and his days were long, but it was satisfying because he was coming home to his family every night. Before long he was able to begin paying his share of the loan every month for his part of the land they were buying.

CHAPTER 24

When Naomi heard that Jonny had bought some land and was planning to move his wife and daughters into a house on the property, her heart leaped for joy. She remembered those days so long ago when things were so uncertain, both for her and for Jonny. She had all but forgotten the hurt and loneliness she had felt that year. It had been nearly five years since Jonny's return from out west. It seemed like every year he had made amazing progress in his life. And she looked back on her own life and saw progress too.

Her little sewing business had grown every year. What began as an experiment to see if she could make a few things had turned into a real business. Harris had changed a lot in those last few years too. Part of that may have been because as her business had grown, she began to believe that she could make it on her own if needed, and she had become more assertive and self-confident. One day she had spent a whole day planning a little speech to him to clear the air.

When he came home from work that evening and all the kids were in bed asleep, she asked him if she could talk to him.

"I know that I haven't been the best wife," she said. "And I can understand that maybe you'd rather have someone else. But if we are to stay together, I need you to be as faithful to me as I am to you. You'll need to make up your mind what you want, because I can't live with you knowing that you are seeking the companionship of other women. If you continue to do that, we'll have to part ways."

"You mean you'd leave me?" he asked.

"Yes," she said. "I think I could make it on my own. Of course, you'd have to help with the kids because they're yours too."

He looked astonished. He always seemed to assume she couldn't do without him. She had felt the same way in times past, but now that her business was a success, she realized she did have a way to support herself even though it would be hard. Harris didn't say much, but she noticed a change in his attitude. He paid more attention to her and seemed to want her approval. He even offered to help her around the house a little. One evening he asked if he could talk to her after the kids were asleep.

"I want to apologize for the things I've done wrong. I know I don't deserve forgiveness, but I'd like you to consider setting aside your grievances for the next three months. If I can win you back, I want us to stay together."

At first Naomi couldn't believe him. She thought it was just a ruse to get her to think he was not being unfaithful. But she decided to at least listen to him.

"So how do you plan to change?"

"Well, for one thing, I plan to be home in the evenings. I've been trying to do that more lately, but I could do better. I would also like to spend more time with you, as I should have been doing all along."

Naomi looked at him. "Okay, I have noticed some differences over the last few months. If that's what you want, we'll try again."

The next three months he really seemed to change. He even got a babysitter to stay with the kids and took her out to supper a few times. He listened to her and respected her opinions about matters they discussed. After about a month she realized he had been home just after work every day and seemed to have no interest in spending time away from his family. Their relationship improved, and the old hurts began to dissolve.

As she walked toward her mother's house one morning, Naomi found herself feeling happier than she had been in years. Watching her kids grow and her husband seeming to enjoy their family made her optimistic. All the kids were in school now, and she still enjoyed her little sewing business.

CHAPTER 25

Jonny came home on a Friday from laying pipelines all day in Rockcastle County. Ellie was busy in the kitchen. After asking if she needed any help, he talked to her a few minutes and then went into the living room and sat down on the couch and began reading his Bible. He read in Matthew, "Seek first his kingdom and his righteousness, and all these things will be given to you as well." The words reminded him of those he'd heard his mother sing so many times: "He walks with me, and he talks with me."

Jonny's life had settled into what he'd always wanted it to be. He wasn't rich, and he wasn't too well educated, but he could read much better, and he felt like his children could have their basic needs met if he continued to work hard. Most of all, he liked being home with his family. His experiences in Tulsa would always be with him, but he had what he wanted now.

When Joy came into the living room, he picked her up, and she gave him a big hug—just what he needed. In a few minutes both girls were in his lap, and Ellie came in to tell them it was time to eat.

After supper, as Jonny was sitting in the rocking chair with his two- and three-year-old daughters and listening to the Grand Ole Opry, he was at peace with himself. Others might think these were the difficult days, the days when he was tied down with family responsibilities. But he knew these were the happy days, the days when he had a family that loved him and that he loved. His wife and these two little ones were the source of his life and happiness.

Jonny occasionally thought back to when he was "Living on Tulsa Time." He would always thank God for getting him back on track in those days when Kitty was alive. He looked up toward the heavens and said, *Kitty, wherever you are, I thank you for reminding me I would find the source of my happiness within.*

The day he received his certificate for eighth grade, Jonny had thought it was the happiest day of his life. And then when he earned his welder's license, it was another source of accomplishment he never thought he'd have. But now he knew these were just steps along the way, just as the day he married Ellie and the day each of his daughters was born.

Connect with the Author

http://on.fb.me/1HHkUXf
https://www.goodreads.com/author/show/6525216.Merrill_J_Davies
https://merrillblogs.blogspot.com/
https://www.merrilldavies.com/
https://twitter.com/MERRILLDAVIES
http://amazon.com/author/merrilljdavies
Merrill@merrilldavies.com